Ruins of the DRAGON REALM

CONTENT ADVICE

Coarse language: Rare/mild

Violence: moderate-to-high fantasy violence/gore

Sex: references only

Contains references to or descriptions of:

Slavery, blood and gore, scars, fire, corpses/undead.

SHADOW DRAGON SAGA

Ruins of the Dragon Realm (Prequel)
Curse of the Dragon Shadow
Legend of the Dragon Soul
Rise of the Dragon Sworn
Blood of the Dragon Throne
Reign of the Dragon Born
Secret of the Dragon Crown

First Edition
Published by Fairies and Fantasy Pty Ltd 2025
ISBN: 978-1-923433-93-9 (paperback)

www.selinafenech.com

RUINS OF THE
DRAGON REALM
SELINA A FENECH
PREQUEL FOR THE
SHADOW DRAGON SAGA

ELUNDRAE
EIGHT WINDS OC
TAEN HIGHLANDS
Nord Halfort
Heithorn Estate
EYLE TAENESK
Tree Wi
Eldisun Grove
The Grea Wing
Vesland Plains
Dragon Keeps
1. Braigwenkeep (Trade Hub)
2. Nevrynkeep (Mining)
3. Ardahnkeep (Trade Harbor, Old Rolanian Capital)
4. Tjollaskeep (Mining)
5. Salixkeep (Fishing)
6. Ulfrenkeep (Mining)
7. Ylvakeep (Farming)
8. Leskakeep (Farming)
9. Pryshakeep (Farming)
10. Dastmyrkeep (Glass)
11. Tarrickeep (Mining)
12. Gerichkeep (Lumber)
13. Skaellakeep (Farming)
14. Idrakeep (Penal)
15. Hjelzahnkeep (Training)
16. Eslindekeep (Incomplete)
EYLE TAENUSH
Longtail River
Abandoned Quarries
(1)
Lorg Cornis
(11)
Unicorr
WESTERN ALDERKIN DEPTHS
(Ewess Deemfret)
Midsun Dale
(2)
Snowshimmer R
Yeonard's Passage
Vasthome Reach
Sturmfell Peaks
Lorg Blessu
(12)
Lorg Nisk
(10)
Tallesis Shores
(16)
Sut Myrr
EYERSUNN SEA

NORTHERN ALDERKIN DEPTHS
(Nerrun Deemfret)
Gris Hofen
(15)
nborn Range
Stonewing Crest
(4)
CENTRAL ALDERKIN DEPTHS
(Luns Deemfret)
Eishowl Peaks
(6)
Bovin Steppes
(13)
(5)
Unicorn Tears River
he Red Cliffs
SOUTHERN ALDERKIN DEPTHS
(ous Deemfret)
Erst Hofen
Talon Bluffs
(8)
Lorg Sesstra
Lorg Eldstrom
Lorg Draeka
Draeskull Crags
Nord Myrr
(9)
Starris River
(3)
Grand Hofen
Serpents Ruu
EYLE NORDCREST
(14)
Seasong Shores
Mestra's Horn
EASTERN ALDERKIN DEPTHS
(Ilst Deemfret)
DRAEKHAN'S REST
(7)
Etherflame Plains
DRAEKHANHELM
SKYBREAK SEA

ONE

The alarm bell clanged, cracking through the quiet hum of the village, and Riony's gaze shot to the sky.

On the verge of taking a leap into the air, she skidded to a stop at the edge of the great slab of orange-ochre stone, holding on with one hand so she didn't topple over onto the sharp rocks below. She scanned the smokey haze above her, seeking anything large, shadowy ... monstrous.

"Aw, are you scared?" Jorrick, a particularly simpering jerk of an overgrown boy, heckled from the safe ground below where he stood with all the other kids.

Riony tossed messy curls off her face with a flick of her chin. "Me? Never. Unless we count that time you flirted with me. Gotta admit, blood ran cold. I lay awake all night reliving the horror. Haunts me to this day."

"We've all been there." Beside the pointy-faced boy, Kaya giggled out her words.

"Why do you punish us so?" Riony asked.

"You all would be lucky if I made a pass at you!" Jorrick declared boldly, but his voice broke, and his face went beet red. "You're just running your mouth so you don't have to jump."

Riony straightened up, filled with the courage gifted by Kaya's smile.

"I said I could make that jump, and I will." Riony moved back to her starting position.

Bouncing on her toes, she eyed the gap from her ledge to the next. A big jump. One no other kid had been game to try.

Riony wasn't scared, but the muster bell kept ringing, throwing off her concentration. Her audience shuffled and muttered between themselves, their attention turning away.

"Please, come down." Lyrrin looked even smaller than normal from above, standing near the pile of boulders and debris. She wrung her gloved hands in front of her. "We have to go back to Amma and Pabba. We have to hide!"

The kid had recently turned six but was acting more like a baby than ever. Riony's cheeks flared again, and she shot her little sister a quelling glare.

Could you not embarrass me in front of Kaya?

Most of the village's children had gathered around the rockfall that afternoon, since chores were done and there was still energy to spend on mischief.

There weren't many areas to play in the bare-rock patch the village was built on, and at sixteen Riony was too old for the lone swing set, so a big pile of cracked boulders beside a cliff had to suffice.

The fact they'd been told not to play on the jagged, unstable stones only made it better. Riony enjoyed the thrill of climbing and jumping across the rough and rocky surfaces. She loved it even more when the girl who made her heart wallop against her ribs was there watching.

A few of the kids had scattered when the muster bell rang, running home, as they were all meant to. The *clang-clang, clang-clang* still echoed around the quarry walls.

Riony glanced at the sky again, wary.

"She is scared, look! Scared of the shadow dragon!"

"Shut your useless spit-hole, Jorrick," Riony yelled back.

"What if it is though? What if the shadow dragon is

coming?" Lyrrin said.

Kaya rolled her eyes toward the small huts and buildings in the main part of the village. "The idiot on watch probably saw a carrion bird and panicked. This is the fifth time this summer."

And each time, Riony had run home so her family could grab their bags and pack their most precious belongings and hold their breath. Only for nothing to happen.

It's probably just another false alarm. But if it's not ...

Lyrrin's vibrant blue eyes sparkled wetly, shadowed under the heavy hood covering her head, and her lips wobbled.

Riony changed angles, looking for her best way to climb down. "Maybe we should go and check—"

"The shadow dragon has never landed here before, even if that was what the watch saw. And even if it did land, there's nothing in the quarry for it to awaken." Kaya remained still, fearless, arms folded, and earthy, golden-tipped curls spread over her shoulders.

The ground beneath them all was bare, hard stone, all the way to the cliffs and protective palisade surrounding their homes. All the top layers of dirt and stone had been scraped clean from the abandoned quarry, taking with it any buried corpses, anything dead.

"That's *why* it doesn't land here." Jorrick rolled his beady eyes. "That's why our village is safe, and the red-headed bigmouth up there is just using the muster bell as an excuse because she's too scared to jump."

Riony sucked air through her teeth and turned back to the gap. Her toes tensed in leather boots that were becoming too tight on her growing feet, and she leaned into her run-up.

I can do it. I've jumped that far on the ground before. This time there's just nothing beneath me except for pointy boulders and pain. No problem.

"Reee-oh-neeeeeeeee, don't!" Lyrrin's whine drifted up with a gust of smokey wind as Riony burst into motion.

The air tasted sour as she huffed deep breaths. Her feet patted over the stone at a speedy rhythm, and then with a thrust of strong legs she was in the air. The worn fabric of her shirt gusted as she hung for a moment at the peak of her jump, then came down again.

I'm going to make it, I'm going to ... Oh, raze it, I'm not going to—

Riony's shin smashed against the sharp edge of the rock she was meant to land on. Sharp pain slammed into her,

but she didn't have time to think about it as the collision sent her tumbling face forward into rock. Tucking herself into a roll, she avoided leaving a bitemark in the stone and tumbled to a skidding stop.

As much as Riony wanted to lie on her side and breathe through the pain as she worked out whether she'd broken her leg, she reminded herself that Kaya was watching and pushed herself quickly up to her feet.

It was only pain, after all.

Riony had known worse.

She raised her arms high then swept into an exaggerated bow.

There was a bit of half-hearted applause from the kids who remained to watch, but all were too distracted by the continuing bell.

Kaya clapped the loudest. "You made it! I thought for sure you were about to kill yourself."

A frustrated squeal burst from Lyrrin, and her pale face turned bright red. "You shouldn't have done that! You're always doing what you want to do. We're supposed to go home to be safe."

"Go then!" Riony snapped.

The fiery outrage in Lyrrin's eyes could have burned

deeper than dragonflame as the child grunted and then ran off alone.

A pang of guilt tugged at Riony as she lowered herself over the ledge and slid down to ground level.

Lyrrin's overreacting. The others are right. We're safe here.

With her feet back on the ground, Riony tested her weight on her injured leg and it held. No wobbly bones. The sting was real though, and a warm flow of liquid tickled down her shin.

Smirking, Riony lifted her chin to Jorrick. "Your turn next?"

"I'm going to … see about the bell. It doesn't normally keep ringing this long. Seems important," Jorrick grumbled, rolled his eyes, and turned away.

"That's okay. I don't blame you for running away. Maybe ask your amma for some tips on how to not be a coward!" Riony hollered after him.

With the show over, all the others left too. All except Kaya.

Riony forgot her guilt over her sister as she stood alone with the prettiest girl in the village. Kaya had an attractive audacity that came from being one of the town leader's children, even if she was just one of many from

multiple wives.

That man is trying to single-handedly keep this blighted world populated.

And even though Riony historically hadn't liked girls whose names started with K, she found herself liking Kaya. Very much. She tried to neaten her unruly hair that sprung free from its short braid. She cleared her throat as she moved closer.

Kaya smiled conspiratorially. "Did you hurt yourself? That whack was loud enough to echo through the quarry."

"There was a whack? Huh. I didn't feel a thing." Riony hid her limp.

"So ... you don't need anyone to look after you?"

Riony swallowed and found her limp again. "You know, maybe it does hurt a little. If you're offering. Maybe you could carry me home."

Kaya playfully shoved Riony's shoulder, then her fingers lingered on the bronzed skin of her bare upper arm. "Between us, I think you're the one more likely to successfully carry anyone anywhere."

A cold chill tickled down Riony's neck as memories of her time as a slave rushed back. Of the other girl whose name started with K. Of the work that had made her strong.

Of the whippings.

If she survived that place, she could survive anything.

Shaking off the past, Riony put her best smile back on. "Maybe we could just head down to the waterfall and—"

"Kaya! Are you deaf, child?" Drahm marched their way, eyes narrowed on them and the pile of rocky debris at their backs. "What are you doing down here? This is no place to be playing, and the muster bell rings!"

"Sorry, Pabba." Kaya bowed, averting her eyes from both her father and Riony as she rushed away.

The town leader came to a stop. His bulky body, strong from his blacksmithing trade, was marked with sweat and soot. He must have been at his forge when the bell rang.

He waited as Kaya disappeared, then turned his attention to Riony who remained stalled on the spot by disappointment that her time alone with Kaya had ended so abruptly. Taking in the warning in Drahm's expression, she got moving as well, as fast as her injured leg could take her. She didn't want any of that man's attention.

It was a common joke around town if he looked at a girl too long, she'd become his next wife. Whether she wanted it or not.

The late summer sun had Riony sweating as she

hobbled her way between the raised garden beds toward home. The cottages were mostly the same, built from the rose-gold sandstone of the quarry and thatched with straw from the rice paddies.

The stone of the older homes had grayed and faded with time, but Riony's home was new, the freshly cut walls bright and unmarred by the ever-present smoke of dragonfire and funeral pyres.

By the time Riony limped up the threshold to her family's cottage, the ache in her shin had bloomed from a sharp sting to a heavy throb. The door stood wide open, and Riony paused there a moment to bend and rub the pain away. Warm air, thick with the scent of drying hennan and carrowmy, wrapped around her.

Riony's amma knelt beside the hearth, franticly sorting jars of ointments and tinctures into a bag.

Without looking up, Eylin said, "What took you so long? Get your bags packed, quick!"

With a barely stifled groan, Riony shuffled toward her room. Her footsteps fell unevenly.

"You're hurt!" Keen eyes shot toward Riony and her mother was across the room in three swift steps, peering out the doorway with fearful eyes.

The old acorn pendant she always wore shifted into view from under her collar, its wood worn smooth. She touched it, briefly, unconsciously. A worry-born habit.

"What happened? Are they in the village already? Did they rise here?"

"There are no revs, Amma. I'm fine" Riony said, even as her leg threatened to give way under her. "Just a jump gone a little sideways."

Elyin's shoulders relaxed and she tsked, brushing a loose strand of hair behind Riony's ear with gentle fingers. Then her eyes widened again.

"Where's Lyrrin?"

"She's not here?" Riony took the last couple of steps to her and Lyrrin's room, peering in for the child's familiar hooded form. "She left for home before me. She must've taken a long way around, I guess?"

Amma's voice sharpened. "You let her go off alone? With the alarm bell ringing?"

"She's six, not a baby," Riony grumbled. "She's the one that got huffy and ran off."

"That's not like her at all. What did you do?" Her mother shot her a look like only mothers could, the one that scraped the guilt inside her red and raw.

Riony turned away and shrugged.

Eylin said, "She's your responsibility when you're out playing."

Heat bloomed through Riony, scorching her cheeks in a churning mix of shame and fury.

True, Riony was supposed to be looking after Lyrrin. And from the moment Riony had been at the child's birth and stolen the baby to keep her alive, she had felt that responsibility deeply.

But Riony had been a slave her whole life and had already been working for years when she was Lyrrin's age. The kid had it easy growing up outside of dragonlord ownership and didn't need eyes on her every minute.

Like the others said, the village was safe.

Riony snatched up her backpack, making a show of packing her belongings into it with rough, punching motions. "She was out of my sight for barely a few minutes. Can't I even have that time to myself?"

"With the *alarm bell ringing*!" Eylin repeated.

"Nothing is going to happen!" Riony's voice rose to meet her mothers.

Her pabba appeared, ducking low through the doorway. Sweat marred his ivory shirt and dirt from the gardens

darkened his rough hands. "Is everybody ready? The bell is still ringing. Swore I saw something in the sky. I don't think this is a false alarm."

"She doesn't have Lyrrin," Eylin said.

Farrad froze. His eyes, so like Riony's, with a nebulous mixture of greys, blues, and golds, narrowed on her. "You lost your sister?"

"She's not lost! Where could she go?" Riony waved her arms around, gesturing to the village walls all around them, invisible from within their cottage.

"Well, she's not *here*," Eylin said, voice high with worry. "And she's your little sister. You're meant to *look after her*."

"I *do!*" Riony shouted. "I just—"

I just wanted one moment to myself. For myself.

Riony glared at the open bag she'd been stuffing belongings into, chaotic and half-packed already from previous false alarms with a worn blanket, spare tunic, a simple straw doll with a red ribbon tied around its waist.

Riony was too old for dolls now, but it was the first toy she ever really had, made by her pabba when they reached the village. One for her and a matching one for Lyrrin, with a blue ribbon.

Lyrrin's lay on the nearby bed as well, and spurred

by a pang of guilt, Riony grabbed it too and worked on stuffing it into the bag.

There wasn't room for both in her backpack without crushing them.

With a grunt of frustration, Riony thrust the opened bag out of her grasp and Lyrrin's doll fell out onto the floor.

"Riony ..." Her pabba's voice grumbled deeply.

"I'll go find her," Riony muttered.

"Quickly. We can't waste time." Eylin turned back to her packing, pausing to make sure the acorn pendant was still secure around her neck. "Farrad, get the—"

"I know, I know the drill." He dusted off his hands and began shoving wrapped flatbread and jarred beans from the kitchen table into a bag.

Beside Riony's bed, her sword leaned against the wall in pride of place. Once a fine blade, it had become dull-edged and pock-marked over the years since Riony had never known how to care for it properly.

Lyrrin's probably fine. She's just dawdling somewhere.

Riony snatched up her sword, just in case. The weight was comforting as she stuck it through a loop on her belt and darted out the door.

The village pathways were full of murmurs and moving

bodies. Some meandered down to the town hall, the safe place they were all meant to be going. Two young brothers argued nearby, faces red.

"I *saw* it," one said, pointing a finger at the sky. "Wings like sailcloth. I know the shape."

"Could've been a dragonrider," said the other. "Or smoke. It's the heat messing with your eyes."

"You wanna bet your life on that?"

Riony moved faster, pushing through the throbbing pain in her leg. She scanned the main paths, around the town hall, past the blacksmith forge, down to the water reservoir. No Lyrrin.

Chewing her lip, Riony swallowed down the bad feeling in her stomach. Her amma was right. It wasn't like Lyrrin to run off. She was normally a quiet child, calm and content to do as she was told.

"Stars, please don't let your first time being disobedient also be the one time the alarm is real," she muttered.

A flicker of movement caught her eye. A small figure stood by the outer palisade, right up close to the sharpened stakes and watchtower scaffolds.

"Lyrrin!"

Riony rushed over in an uneven limp. Her sister didn't

turn. She stood with her hood up, face pressed to the wood, fingers splayed against the wall.

"What in all that's razed are you doing out here?" Riony hissed as she reached her, grabbing her arm. "Come on, we have to get home before Amma decides maybe our old masters were onto something with their love of whippings."

Beneath Riony's grasp, her sister trembled. She crouched down to Lyrrin's level. "Are you okay? What's wrong?"

"I can hear them," Lyrrin whispered.

Riony's blood turned to ice. "Hear *what*?"

She leaned in to listen—and then caught the faintest rasp.

A dragging sound. A low, hungry groan.

Lyrrin pointed to a crack in between the thick logs of the palisade wall.

Heart pounding, Riony peered through the narrow split. On the other side, half-shrouded by smoke, something moved.

Human shaped, its skin was gray and sloughing, patches of it torn to the sinew. Its mouth opened wide, revealing blackened gums and yellowed teeth.

It raced at Riony, smashing into the wall between them. It clawed at the wood with ragged hands, drawn in a mindless rage toward the scent of life just out of reach.

A revenant.

And it wasn't alone.

TWO

Riony flung herself away from the wall, scrambling backward with a gasp. In a flash she had her sword out in front of her in one hand and Lyrrin clutched behind her with the other.

"Do you think they can get in?" Lyrrin whispered.

Riony pulled her sister a little closer. She took a deep breath and eyed the sturdy palisade, built from trunks of the tall pines that grew in the surrounding forest.

The revenants probably couldn't get in. Probably. But that didn't change the fact that there were ravenous, risen corpses, right there, clawing and snarling at the barrier between them. Undead that wouldn't rest until they reached their prey.

Riony grabbed for Lyrrin's gloved hand. "The shadow dragon must have come to land somewhere nearby. We have to warn the others."

Riony tried to move, but Lyrrin's hand pulled back. The child was stuck to the spot, mouth open in a silent scream. Her little face was turned to the sky, and Riony's gaze followed.

A dark shape swooped low toward them. Air whooshed beneath leathery wings and scarlet scales shimmered in the golden light.

Heat shimmered and crackled in the creature's toothy maw.

"Watch out!" Riony yelled, both to Lyrrin and the dragonrider she glimpsed on top of the etherflame's back.

Her warning fell uselessly as the dragon shot its breath of fire their way.

Riony heaved Lyrrin up into her arms and launched two long strides away from the wall. Her injured leg screamed. The jet of flame rushed down behind her. Heat flushed her from heels to shoulder blades as she dropped to the ground, covering Lyrrin with her body.

The fire hit the palisade wall, scorching down both

sides. From the outer side, gargling inhuman cries tore through the air and then cut out.

By the time Riony had decided she wasn't burning alive and rolled off Lyrrin to lie panting on her back, other villagers were running in with buckets of water to save their wooden defenses.

"What in the stars happened?" Alhar, one of Drahm's older sons, paused by Riony and offered her a hand up.

She begrudgingly took it then turned away from his dark, lingering gaze to help up her sister.

"Revs," Riony coughed out. "There were revs outside the wall, and …"

"There's a rider! A rider saved us!" a voice called from nearby.

The air whooshed around them, stirring up sparks and dust as the dragonrider on his red etherflame circled back around.

"You almost burned us alive, you ass-faced, chowder-brained jerk!" Riony hollered at the sky.

Her curses were drowned out by applause from the other villagers.

Sure, cheer on the man who almost killed me and Lyrrin and who set our palisade alight.

Riony glared at the man in his glimmering dragonscale armor as he brought his beast down to land in a clear section beside the cottages. She lifted an arm over her face to shield from the flurry of dust from the dragon's landing.

They were all the same, dragonriders. She'd never known any that weren't cruel, selfish monsters. At least, every one at Heithorn Estate had been back when Riony's family were slaves there. It had only made sense that the youngest of the dragonlord family had been so obsessed with becoming one herself, considering what an awful gremlin Kess was.

People were flooding in now, crowding around the extinguished, smoking palisade and the dragonrider, dismounting from his saddle.

"Look at it!" Lyrrin whispered in awe.

"What? It's just an etherflame." Riony kept her eyes narrowed on the beast.

The most common species, the tamed creature sat dull and motionless now that its rider wasn't taking control. Riony shivered. She hated the glazed, mindless look dragon's eyes held. The taming spike in its forehead glinted in the afternoon light.

"It's sooo cute though! I want to pat it!" Lyrrin cooed,

tugging Riony's hand to move closer.

"Of course you do." Riony half-smiled. The kid's love of animals knew no reason or limit.

Lyrrin's gloved hand slipped out of Riony's and her slight, six-year-old body slipped away through the crowd toward the dragon like an eel through water.

"Hey, wait!" Riony made chase, groaning on her aching leg and having to shoulder through people to catch up.

Before they reached the thickest part of the crowd, Lyrrin was snatched from her path.

"Pabba!" she squealed, her hood falling back as she was lifted into his arms.

"Are you two okay?" Eylin rushed in beside the girls.

She scanned over Riony then turned to Lyrrin, stroking her cheek before pulling her hood back up over her dyed dark hair. "My little moon."

As people jostled around them, Riony noticed Kaya stepping in at her side.

"We're fine, you don't have to worry so much," she hissed at her mother under her breath, rolling her eyes and stepping away from her parents concerned looks.

"Did I hear someone say there were revs?" Farrad asked.

"I saw them!" Lyrrin chirped. "Well, I heard them but

then Riony stole my peephole, and I didn't get to see them and then the dragon rider burned them up!"

"Oh wow," Kaya breathed the words, bright eyes looking toward where the dragon's folded wings and arched neck were visible above a sea of heads.

From within the center of the crowd, a deep voice rose. "You're all safe! I've taken care of the revenants. There was a rising nearby, but those couple I chased here were the last of them. No need to fear."

A younger, higher voice replied, "I told you I saw the shadow dragon fly by!"

The enthusiastic bell ringer, Riony figured, since the bell had now stopped ringing.

Drahm's familiar tone boomed through the crowd. "We are in your debt, Sir ..."

"Call me Veyrn. This is a nice place you've got here. Interesting location."

"I can't see." Kaya was up on her tip-toes, pouting and craning to see over the crowd.

"Hey, come with me." Riony touched Kaya's arm and gestured for her to follow.

She moved through the few people on the outskirts and headed to the nearest cottage.

"This way." Riony stepped up onto the edge of a barrel and reached back a hand to pull Kaya up beside her. "And up again."

The sloped, thatched roof wasn't far above their heads, and Riony bent low, lacing her fingers together for Kaya to step into them. Then she stood strong, boosting the girl onto the eaves of the cottage. Kaya leaned stomach first onto the roof then threw one knee up then another until she was kneeling on the edge.

Her tunic fluttered in the light breeze. And she turned a pink-cheeked face into the wind, her mouth parted.

Riony followed, grasping the under beam of the structure and pulling her body up in a fluid, strong motion. Her own cheeks warmed with the low-lidded way Kaya watched her.

Wincing as her sore leg took her weight, she grabbed for the peak of the roof and climbed up the scratchy straw. Once settled straddled over the top, she reached back again.

Kaya squealed softly, wobbling on the thatching.

"You're alright, I've got you." Riony squeezed the warm hand in hers, and Kaya smiled at her in a breathless way that turned all of Riony's insides into aching lava.

"You're so strong." Kaya took a seat on the ridge beside

Riony, their shoulders touching.

Riony liked to stay strong and worked hard to do so, because her strength had saved her life and others in the past. But she also liked that it made Kaya look at her like that.

Riony smirked and flexed an arm. "I can show you some of my other muscles too if you like. Happy to show you anything you want."

Kaya wheezed a laugh. "You're cute, but a word of advice?"

"Sure."

"Don't come on so strong with this silly flirting thing you do. It might turn some people off."

Silly? Riony's churning insides cooled significantly. "Right. Sure. Okay."

Kaya leaned into her again, bumping shoulders with a smile. "Trust me, you're doing fine without saying any of that stuff."

As the renewed heat in Riony burned away her words, Kaya gasped. "Oh, this is a great view!"

Riony tore her gaze away from the only thing she really wanted to look at toward the view below. Over the crowd, the town leader, Drahm, was clearly visible in the center along with the dragonrider and his dragon.

In the distance, a column of dark smoke rose to the sky, adding to the haze.

Must have been where the shadow dragon landed. The rider really set the place alight.

"I want to see too," a small voice called from below.

"Go back with Amma and Pabba," Riony called out. Then said more quietly to Kaya, "Sorry. My sister is so annoying."

Kaya's eyes glittered. "No, it's cute how you look after her."

Riony cleared her throat and turned to climb back down. "I'll go help her up."

Small, gloved hands were grasping then slipping off the eaves, followed by frustrated grunts each time Lyrrin landed back on the barrel.

Riony looked down as Lyrrin was tugging the glove off one hand.

She hissed roughly. "Stop it! Leave them on. You know you can't take them off outside!"

"I can't climb with them on." Lyrrin stuck out her bottom lip but obediently pulled the glove back into place again.

Sighing, Riony dropped back down beside her. She squatted, facing away from her sister.

"Go on, hop on."

Lyrrin flung her arms around Riony's neck with a light giggle, and Riony climbed them both back up to the ridge of the cottage.

"Sit over there." Riony pointed toward the other end of the ridge away from her and Kaya. "And don't move. Amma and Pabba will have that dragon chew me up me if you fall."

Lyrrin let go of Riony and nodded, but her startling blue eyes were already on the dragon and she sat down right at Riony's side. She pulled one of Riony's hands into hers and held it, patting it with gloved fingers like it was a pet.

"Wow, look at it!" Lyrrin grinned widely.

Riony had to remind herself that Lyrrin hadn't grown up around dragons and their lords and riders the way she had. She'd seen so few in her life, especially up close. The massive beasts were common to Riony, but she could see how impressive they were, with fresh eyes.

The etherflame's scales were a deep red down its spine, fading out to a more rose gold tone on its chest. Its folded wings draped like heavy cloth, spotted in a delicate lacework pattern. Muscled limbs ended with talons like sickles, and the points of long teeth showed white and gleaming along the edges of its closed mouth.

Its wedge-shaped head hung on a bent neck, and it remained still as a statue, only the rise and fall of its shoulders showing it was alive and breathing.

Lyrrin's smile dropped a little. "Why isn't it moving at all?"

Riony said the obvious in a tone that said it was obvious. "It's *tamed*."

Lyrrin's head shook as though she didn't understand. "It seems so sad."

"Forget the dragon, how about the rider? He's so handsome in that scale armor," Kaya said. "And so heroic, saving us like that!"

Riony wanted to argue, point out how close she'd come to being caught up in the same fire that took out the revs, which wasn't a very heroic thing for the rider to have done. Also, that the rider certainly wasn't handsome at all. But the conversation below started up again, reaching them clearly from their vantage point, and Kaya shushed her.

"I didn't realize you all were out here. Since I followed the revs here, I figured I'd stop in, see how your little

community is fairing," the dragonrider said.

"Thriving, as you can see." Drahm swept an arm around to show off the mass of villagers, probably half of which were his children and grandchildren.

The blacksmith could be a strict leader at times, but despite his penchant for breeding, he was still way better than Riony's masters at her last home.

They could never go back there anyway, even if they wanted to. Only the noose would await them there after what they did when they escaped.

Lyrrin shuffled beside Riony, slipping on the thatching. Riony put an arm around her, pulling her a bit closer.

"No dragonrider protection though?" Veyrn looked about, as though checking for any dragons they had hidden away behind the low cottages.

"Our walls and location have kept us safe so far."

Veyrn turned to take in the barren stone ground. "Good idea setting up in a quarry. I knew the owners of this place, you know. Worked for them back before it closed. It's got quite the history."

Drahm leaned into the man, whispering something and patting him on the shoulder. "You know, it wouldn't hurt to have some support from a dragon rider. If you're from a base nearby, maybe we could come to an arrangement, now you know we're here?"

Riony scoffed under her breath. What did they need a dragonrider's protection for? The revs couldn't get in. And any that did find their way there to scratch at their outer walls could have been dealt with another way.

Veyrn leaned back, his face a mask of commiseration. "Ah, I would love to, but I'm in the hire of Braigwenkeep. It's my duty to keep the people of that dragonkeep and its surrounds safe. A small settlement like yours … doesn't have the same resources, you understand."

Drahm pushed in closed again with a strange eagerness. "I'm sure we could find some way to compensate you."

Veyrn's gaze narrowed with a sly smile, and he looked out around the people, still fawning over him and his dragon. The crowd had thinned some now, with a number of people dispersing since the danger and excitement had passed. Including Riony's parents.

Riony leaned forward and rubbed her sore leg, looking forward to getting home herself and being able to treat it with one of her mother's herbal remedies.

"Still sore? You big baby." Kaya trilled a giggle.

The rider's eyes lifted to them, taking in Riony and

Kaya, sitting side by side on the roof, and his smile widened.

He leaned close to Drahm, speaking in his ear.

Drahm frowned, bushy brows darkening his soot-stained face. He whispered in reply, a short to and fro passing between them until Drahm shrugged and smiled, patting the rider on the back with a hearty slap.

Veyrn turned again toward Riony, his eyes lingering on her in a way that chilled her surer than a plunge under the waterfall.

Dragonriders only ever cared about themselves. Riony didn't believe for a moment that he was going to help protect their village. And she didn't like the way he was looking at her at all.

THREE

A frantic pounding at the front door shook Riony out of her meditative work. She dropped the sprigs of dried hennan she was stripping leaves from into the basket and pushed her chair back to open the door.

Lyrrin rushed past her and grabbed the handle.

"Gloves!" Eylin snapped.

"Who's beating our door down at this hour?" Farrad moved past the candle on the corner of the table where Riony had been working, making the flame flicker.

Lyrrin groaned, running back to the shared bedroom with her clawed fingers clenched into fists. Riony slipped around her to steal the glory of opening the door.

"Riony!" Kaya's flushed face greeted her, eyes twinkling in the low light of sunset. "Come on, come on! The dragonrider is coming back!"

Kaya grabbed Riony's hands and was tugging her out of the cottage before the words sank in.

"You have work to finish." Eylin placed a hand on Riony's shoulder.

Riony's jaw tensed caught between the two forces pulling at her. She whispered like a plea, *"Amma."*

Eylin looked sympathetic but didn't remove her hand. "I have to keep an eye on dinner, but we need those herbs processed and bottled before they lose their potency. You know we need them for Lyrrin."

"He's landing now! If we hurry we can see the dragon up close." Kaya bounced in place, shaking Riony's arm up and down.

Riony didn't care much about the dragon but didn't want Kaya to let go of her. She shifted forward, tugging her shoulder free of her mother's grasp.

"I'll be back soon and finish my work then."

"Ri—" Farrad called from behind as Riony raced away.

There was a squeal from Lyrrin—hopefully being intercepted before she could follow Riony and Kaya as well.

Heart racing, Riony ran hand in hand with Kaya toward the center of the village where the blacksmith forge shed a warm red light through its open door.

A grin spread on Riony's face as the disturbed air from the dragon's landing tossed her curls. Kaya giggled as they hustled and pushed to the very front of the crowd.

Fewer people had gathered this time, since the muster bell wasn't ringing and evening was falling. Drahm barked orders to the strongest in that group, getting them to work unloading canvas wrapped supplies the dragon had carried in its claws.

"I can help move some things." Riony stepped forward, rolling her sleeves up with a slight glance back at Kaya to make sure she was watching.

Drahm corralled her back beside him. "That's all right, we've enough helpers. You stay here with me."

His heavy, sooty hand rested heavily on her shoulder, keeping her beside him. Riony's eyebrows raised, and she shot a look at Kaya to see if she could explain the situation, but Kaya just shrugged and turned back to watch the rider dismounting.

"He makes it all look so easy," she breathed in awe. "It's amazing."

Veyrn came over to join them, and Kaya straightened up at Riony's side, tucking her flowing hair behind one ear and curtseying slightly.

Riony remained still, showing as much blatant disdain on her face as she dared in such close proximity to both the town leader and a man who could have her swallowed by his steed on a whim.

"The mirror array, as requested." Veyrn waved a hand back at the bundles packaged roughly in canvas and rope. "The newest technology and best way to signal for dragonrider assistance. Work this contraption right, and riders all across Elundrae will see your distress signal."

Drahm called over one of the women carrying a parcel and peeled back the wrapping to reveal some battered metal and glass darkened with soot.

Riony scoffed under her breath.

Doesn't look very new to me. Where did this guy scrounge this rubbish up from?

Heithorn estate never had a signaler. They had their own riders so didn't need to call in more for help. But Riony had heard of them from her rider-obsessed master. They were common enough even six years ago.

Drahm, however, puffed up with how pleased he

seemed. "Wonderful, wonderful! I'm so glad we can rely on you, in the case we ever were to need it."

"Always happy to make a deal." Veyrn smiled, and although he spoke to Drahm, his gaze drifted to Riony and stayed there.

Drahm's voice lowered. "And the other thing?"

Veyrn leaned in with a wink and pointed to a small keg, painted red around the rim.

Then he smiled at Riony again. "All sorted. You'll have no problems."

Drahm flagged down one of his helpers and sent them with the small barrel toward the forge.

Veyrn inhaled sharply. "Do be careful where you store it though."

Clearing his throat, Drahm redirected the barrel over to a storage area behind the town hall.

"And our arranged payment?"

Drahm's grasp on Riony tightened. "This is Riony Uf'Heithorn—"

"*That* is *not* my name anymore!" Riony hissed in outrage.

Drahm continued talking right over her, pushing her forward toward the rider. "—and she is honored to be

introduced to you."

"Introduced? Wait … *Payment?*" Riony sputtered, shaking off Drahm's grip as she connected dots she didn't want to. "Oh no, you are razing tamebrained if you think you can *introduce* me into any kind of *payment arrangement*."

"Pabba, what's going on?" Kaya whispered.

"It's a wonderful opportunity, child, imagine the life you could have with such a man." Drahm's voice was cordial, but low and filled with warning.

Riony's head was too filled with raging fire to hear it. "I know exactly what kind of life that would be, and you can both ram it up your asses with the spikey end of a dragon's tail, because you would have to drag my still warm carcass out to be reanimated by the shadow dragon before I go anywhere with a dragonrider."

A murmur rippled through the bystanders, echoes of the word payment and questions passing between them. But nobody stepped forward. Nobody challenged Drahm.

"Is she always this mouthy?" The dragonrider's smug smile remained. He reached out, looping a finger through a red lock at Riony's cheek. "She's easy on the eyes but I don't like the noisy ones."

Riony jerked away, snarling like a rabid revenant. "Touch me again and I'll show you how mouthy my fists can get too."

Drahm's hand was back on Riony's shoulder, shaking her as though that could bring her into agreement. But Veyrn waved a hand casually at him.

"She looks like trouble. What about that one?" He tilted his head toward Kaya.

Drahm's eyes flashed over his daughter as she stared back at him, wide eyed and confused. "That's ... well, that is ..."

Veyrn tutted softly. "If we don't have an agreement anymore, I'm sure I can find another settlement looking for a signaler."

"Of course. Of course. Kaya is wonderful, and you'll find her very obedient."

"Pabba?" Kaya whispered.

"What? No!' Riony snapped.

Drahm smiled and shushed Kaya gently. "Don't you like this charming dragonrider? Come, get to know him a bit more."

"I suppose. I have wanted to meet him." Kaya took a tentative step forward. Her lips were a mix of polite smile

and confused frown.

Drahm's smile grew. "That's right. And you're old enough that we were going to find a match for you soon anyway, you knew that. And look what a fine match we've found."

Riony snarled again, but an arm, firm and familiar, wrapped around her and pulled her back.

"What's happening?" Riony's father whispered into her ear.

His presence, the warm earth smell he always held from his days tending the crops, broke through Riony's fury to the childlike fear buried beneath. Tears flushed her eyes but didn't fall.

"He's going to take her. He's going to take her," she whispered back in a rush.

He almost took me.

Kaya didn't know. She didn't understand. She hadn't grown up around dragonriders and lords, she hadn't been a slave before, hadn't had every part of her body and life owned and abused by others. The scars on Riony's back burned and itched.

Kaya smiled sweetly, moving a little closer to Veyrn. "Do you think we could—"

"I really don't have time for this." Veyrn clicked his fingers toward Kaya and moved back toward his dragon. "I don't like flying in the dark. Let's get going."

"Going? Now? I have to leave with him?" Kaya's voice raised into a high squeak. "I haven't ... I should say goodbye to Amma, my sisters."

Veyrn paused by his dragon's shoulder and called back to Drahm, "Will she be trouble if I take her up in the saddle with me, or should we bind her and have the dragon carry her?"

"She'll be no trouble. None at all." Drahm herded Kaya over to Veyrn's side, urging her to climb up after him.

Kaya moved stiffly, her lips parted and eyes wide as she looked out over the crowd, as though seeking her family, seeking answers, seeking one final look at the village she grew up in. But she climbed, and Veyrn pushed her into place in the saddle behind him on the dragon's shoulders.

"They can't." Riony lunged forward, struggling in Farrad's hold. "Kaya!"

Her father's strong arms kept her in place as the dragon's wings stretched and flapped and the crowd moved away from the swirling dust.

And just like that, Kaya was gone, and Riony was left

staring at the bruised dusky sky with her chest heaving and eyes burning and a deep, heavy sorrow that told her she'd never see Kaya again.

"Drahm, what was that? What did you do?" Cyra, the oldest woman in town, pointed a crooked finger at the town leader.

A few others added their voices to hers, demanding answers.

"This is what I've done," Drahm gestured to the wrapped bundles Veyrn had brought them. "I've provided safety and security for our village for years to come. We will all be able to thrive without fear of the shadow dragon. Think how better off we will be with the ability to call for dragonrider assistance, if, given the small chance, revenants make it into our settlement."

Cyra tutted softly, tilting her head toward the broken junk the rider had provided. "Those revs did get awfully close the other day."

"And if they'd gotten in, we got no dragon of our own to burn them," a voice from further in the crowd added.

The low hum of outrage ebbed away before it had even risen more than a voice.

Riony's still burned blistering hot.

Still held firm by her father, she yelled, "And what about Kaya?"

Drahm's eyes flashed briefly, and his barrel chest rose and fell and his smile returned. "She will have the safety of life in a dragonkeep under a rider's protection. What could be better than that?"

"She'll be a slave!" Riony's voice broke over the word.

A few of the dispersing villagers threw pitying looks Riony's way, and she couldn't even tell if they cared about Kaya or were pitying her for missing out on what Drahm was selling as a golden opportunity. But for them, the excitement was over. For them, a business arrangement had been made that would benefit them all.

Riony slumped in Farrad's grip. She'd never see Kaya again. And it was almost her. She wouldn't have been able to say goodbye to her parents, to Lyrrin. Would they have fought for her? Tried to get her back? Or accepted the trade and new status quo and moved on like everyone else was doing now?

Drahm remained in front of her and Farrad, the only people remaining in the now dark street.

Riony growled low, "You sold your daughter's life for a pile of scrap and glass."

"I made an arrangement that will be better for all of us. She will live in luxury and we will be able to stay safe here. And you, you almost ruined it!" Drahm's genial façade broke and spittle flew at Riony as he growled back.

"It was a *small* trade in return for *all* of our lives here."

"She's your daughter!"

Drahm snapped his gaze away from Riony and up to Farrad above her. "And you need to work harder to control yours. Kaya knew her place, knew that we all must do what we can for the greater good. Our safety depends upon numbers, and the value each number of us can provide, and there will always be sacrifices."

Farrad's grip on Riony tightened, and he stared Drahm down, only offering a small grunt in reply, not negative, but hardly in agreement either.

Drahm continued, "But we all must do our part! And I've given you newcomers some leeway, but it's time you all did more after what you just cost me." Drahm jabbed a sooty finger Riony's way. "We lost one today, and we always need more. Growing our numbers is our best chance for survival. Unfortunately, Eylin is no doubt too old for more children now."

Farrad tensed but said nothing.

Riony also tensed at the idea of having more younger siblings to care for but wasn't too worried about it. She knew for sure her mother's cycle had already ended.

Eylin had told Riony once that she'd never intended on having children.

"Bring a child into this world? Feels like cruelty," she'd said.

She was already older than usual when Riony came as a late accident, and then Lyrrin was something else entirely.

But whether or not Eylin could have children anymore hadn't removed the sly grin growing on Drahm's lips. "Yes, she's probably too old, but Riony here isn't too young."

"*Drahm*," Farrad warned.

The town leader held up a hand to ward off his objections. "My son Alhar recently lost his wife in childbirth, something Eylin failed to prevent—"

"She did everything she could," Riony snapped back.

She knew. She was there, assisting her mother. She'd seen the blood, so much blood, that just wouldn't stop. She and Eylin had sat with the woman, letting her hold her newborn baby as she took her last, weakened and spent breath.

"Eylin is a capable midwife, I'll give her that, but my son

is still without a partner, and Riony is of child birthing age."

Farrad shook his head. "She's sixteen, your son is more than twice her age and she doesn't even want—"

"It doesn't matter what she wants. We all make sacrifices for the greater good here. We need to replace lost numbers, replace the service Kaya would have done for our community. Riony *will* take her role, or there is no place in the safety of our village for your family."

FOUR

"There is no razing way in this forsaken world that I'm going to become part of Drahm's baby farm." Riony burst through her front door, pushing it so hard it slammed into the wall.

At the hearth, Eylin startled at the crashing sound, her expression one that told Riony she was in for a scolding for how she'd run off before. But when her mother's gaze passed over Riony's reddened eyes and how Farrad kept his arm around her, her expression shifted to something softer, questioning.

"What's going on?" Lyrrin whined from beside the

table. Her dyed, dark hair was a wild tangle from being kept under a hood so often.

Riony's teeth clenched, and she couldn't get her words out.

"A few things," Farrad replied.

"What's a baby farm?" Lyrrin asked.

"Drahm plans to have Riony married to his son, Alhar," Farrad answered, but looked to his wife more than Lyrrin.

Eylin's lips pulled tight.

"But Riony doesn't even like boys. That's silly." Lyrrin rolled her eyes and turned away as though that finished the matter.

"Tell me what happened." Eylin placed a lid over the cooking pot and took it off the fire.

Wiping her hands on her apron, she took a seat at the table. Lyrrin moved to her side, cuddling one of her arms and watching the conversation with wide eyes.

Riony slumped into a chair beside her mother and out flowed an entire re-enactment.

"He was going to give me to the rider! He hadn't even asked, hadn't said anything, just tried to hand me over! But I told them explicitly what I thought of that, and then the rider didn't want me anymore."

"Good girl," Farrad mussed a hand through Riony's hair.

Eylin tutted under her breath about Farrad encouraging Riony's recklessness. Louder, she said, "Drahm thinks he owns this place and everyone in it to spend as he wishes."

"So I don't have to marry his son, right?"

Eylin half-nodded, giving her husband a questioning look. "Surely we can talk Drahm out of this."

"He seemed pretty set. You know what he's like."

"It's not. Going. To. Happen." Riony slammed her fist on the table with each word. "We should leave. Go and live somewhere without some tyrant playing dragonlord thinking he owns all of us."

Eylin sighed deeply. "Good luck finding such a place. You remember what it was like with the Heithorn's. And out in the blighted world before we found this settlement. Life *out there* is no life at all. We need the safety this village provides."

Riony's heartrate sped up.

Safety. All they cared about was safety. Would they trade Riony's life and body for that safety?

Her pitch rose as she pled, "I heard Jorrick talking about an underground city in the mountains, where lots

of people have been going. It's safe from revs and dragons. We could go there."

Eylin's frown deepened. "And live underground? I've heard rumors of that place too. I'm not taking my family to live in the dark."

"I'll go on my own if I have to," Riony growled.

"You'd leave us?" Lyrrin whimpered.

Eylin rubbed the child's back and locked eyes with Riony. "Of course she wouldn't. She knows how important she is to you. She understands her responsibilities."

Riony broke eye contact, looking down.

Farrad slapped a hand onto Riony's back. "Don't worry, love. We'll work something out. We can make anything happen if we work hard enough. Remember, big dreams, bold deeds."

"Big dreams, bold deeds!" Lyrrin chirped an echo.

Riony rolled her eyes. She wasn't sure any of them were dreaming big, just trying to stay alive and out of arranged marriages in their little walled in settlement. Maybe that was enough. It was certainly better than life at the Heithorn's was, with their cruel masters and the whipping post.

But even then, her parents had been content to stay

in the safety of being owned slaves, despite how many whippings their mouthy daughter took.

Their days on the run with Lyrrin after that had been hard in the scorched and wild wastelands. Hiding from revenants and marauders and scrounging up enough food to keep them going. But at least they'd been free.

Riony lifted her gaze again to find her mother's worried eyes still on her. A hard line had formed between her brows, and one arm was tight around Lyrrin.

The child that Riony's reckless actions had brought into their family. That Riony was responsible for, even if that responsibility grated against her.

Riony knew she couldn't let her actions take Lyrrin into the dangers outside their village walls.

"We'll work something out," Eylin repeated, but her words sounded airy and weak.

Riony nodded. Because one way or another, she knew she would not marry Drahm's son.

Every day for five days Riony's parents met with Drahm, trying to change his mind. Every conversation only seemed to make Drahm more adamant, bringing the arranged marriage closer and closer.

The ceremony would be perfunctory, but still a

necessary step in making the rest of the village think this was even half-way toward a consensual relationship. They would be getting the basics. And it would be happening tomorrow.

Riony pressed her back to the wall of the forge. The stone was warm from the fires burning inside, and Riony's cheeks burned hotter from the conversation she eavesdropped on.

"Your child's rude mouth cost me a daughter." Drahm's voice drifted around the corner.

Farrad snapped back, "Only because you tried to sell our daughter off in secret!"

Eylin's tone was painstakingly reasonable and calm. "Whatever happened is done. But we can still work together to make sure we're all happy here."

A harsh scoff. "Riony will be happy with Alhar. She should be happy to do her part for the longevity of our settlement."

More calm words. "She can be a productive member of our community without becoming a wife and mother at this age. She has both midwife and herbalism training, and she regularly works the gardens with Farrad. She contributes plenty."

"She cost me a daughter, so she will take that place and make me grandchildren." Drahm didn't yell. Instead, his voice grew venomously low. "This discussion is ended, or the lot of you will be packed up and put out the gates."

A heavy door slammed. A groan and deep sigh came from Riony's parents.

"That man is unreasonable, him and his ... his ... *baby farm*," Eylin hissed.

"I could kill him in his sleep tonight if that helps," Farrad offered in a low grumble.

Riony half smiled at her father's offer.

Eylin tsked. "She gets her recklessness from you."

"You mispronounced bravery."

"Bravery that has gotten us into troubles after troubles."

Riony's heart sank. Her parents had never outright blamed her for the Lyrrin situation or any other. But she knew she'd made life harder for them all.

Hearing it confirmed was a lash to the heart. Riony slouched against the wall.

"You'd prefer Riony was taken away by that dragonrider without us ever even seeing her go? You'd prefer we didn't have Lyrrin?"

"Of course not." Eylin exhaled loudly. "I just wish

she'd understand her responsibilities more. Lyrrin needs her, and she's running off with friends getting into trouble like this."

There was a rustle of fabric below her father's deep grumble. "Come on now. Don't you remember what it was like at that age? She just wants some freedom, some control over her own life. We ask a lot of her, and she's just a kid."

"The world is more dangerous now than when we were that age. And Drahm and his son are going to ask a razing lot more of Riony than we do." Riony's mother's voice broke. "Stars. I don't know how to keep protecting our children in this world."

Her last words were muffled. Riony peeked around the corner to see her parents in a tight embrace. Farrad whispered soft words of comfort in his wife's ear.

He released her again, and Riony hid back around the corner.

"We *could* run," Eylin offered. "We'd be in a better starting position than when we left the Heithorn's. At least we can pack supplies this time. Braigwenkeep isn't too far. We could sell the silvernix, buy our way in and get settled there. It will be harder keeping Lyrrin hidden in a city, but ..."

The words faded out with departing footsteps.

Riony shook her head to herself.

They can't sell the silvernix. It's too precious.

That single drop of unicorn blood was enough to save a life. One of their lives. In Riony's mind, it felt like swapping a life for safety all over again.

There had to be another way to stop the marriage going ahead.

As the afternoon sun dropped lower, spreading a flaming orange blaze across the sky, Riony skirted around the back of the blacksmith's. Most of the other villagers finished up their work for the day, heading home. Drahm would have to soon as well.

Across an open area to Riony's left, the signaler now stood in the center of the village. The tower stood on a spindly metal framework, slightly crookedly, whether from the dodgy materials or poor construction.

The wide dish mirror sat like a mushroom cap on top, with a couple of levers and cranks to adjust the angle to best catch the light. A rough hessian cover was thrown over the mirror, keeping it from sending flashes of light into the sky when not intended.

Riony glowered at the structure. Having it there had

made most of the town happier and more carefree.

"Just in case," they would say. "Just in case some rev gets in. Not that they will. But just in case. Nice to know we'd have dragonriders on the way."

Nobody spoke again about what it had cost them.

It seemed as though everyone had forgotten about Kaya. But Riony hadn't.

Riony understood sacrifice. About doing something bold, even reckless, when needed. But such sacrifice should always be a choice, and that fate wasn't Kaya's choice.

And it's not my choice to marry Alhar and start popping out babies.

Riony shuddered.

As a midwife and practical woman, Riony's mother had never spared Riony from any detail about the pregnancy and birth process.

Absolutely not.

The click of a latch came from around the corner, and Riony leaned out a little to see Drahm leaving his forge, heading home for the day.

With a few swift, silent steps, Riony ducked around the side of the blacksmiths and pushed the front door. It swung open—few in their small village felt the need to lock their buildings. Least of all their undisputed leader.

Riony scanned around the space, lit in dim red tones from the dying forge. Somewhere amongst the farming tools awaiting repair and anvils and pliers and oily buckets and singed rags, somewhere, there must be something Riony could use.

She wasn't sure exactly what she might find. Something secret or dirt she could blackmail the town leader with into stopping the arranged marriage would be ideal.

Or even just finding some way to stuff up his life and make it miserable too would be a consolation.

A rustle of movement in the corner had Riony reaching for her sword—which she wasn't wearing. Breath caught in her throat. She glared into the darkness at a black metal cage.

Beady eyes stared back, fixed between a sickle-sharp beak. The mangy sparrow-vulture let out a husky caw, throwing itself at the bars.

Only as long as Riony's forearm, the creature was ugly and ragged. It rattled its cage with strong bites of its beak and scrapes from long taloned claws, as eager to carve into its prey as a revenant.

Kaya had told Riony how her father liked keeping the

violent creature around, as a display of his power. She said he'd have liked to get a full-sized carrion bird if he could.

Riony hissed, "Shut it, you nasty thing!"

"What are you doing?"

Riony jumped clear out of her skin at the voice behind her. She spun to match the small, high voice with the face it belonged to.

"Stars dammit! Lyrrin? You're meant to be at home."

Lyrrin looked more suited to sneaking around than her older sister, with her hood shadowing her face and gloves over her hands. "So are you. Amma and Pabba told you to stay and look after me. But you didn't stay, so I figured if I stay with you then you can look after me here."

She finished brightly, as though she'd come up with a perfect solution worthy of praise.

"But what are we doing *here*?" Lyrrin looked about the blacksmith's shop skeptically, only smiling when she saw the awful vulture. "Ooh, a birdy!"

"Nothing. We're leaving." Riony grabbed Lyrrin's shoulders and turned her around, pushing her back toward the door.

More voices from the other side froze her in place.

"If you have something to say, you can speak to me

in here."

Drahm.

Riony's head swiveled. The barrels were too close to the wall to hide behind. The anvil too small to cover her and Lyrrin. She tilted her head back.

Squatting down briefly, she scooped Lyrrin into one arm and hissed, "hold tight!"

She stepped onto a low wooden crate, then up onto the edge of a water barrel, leaving the contents sloshing. Jumping from there, she got one hand grasped around a beam of the high rafters. The wood was covered in thick soot, making her hand slip. She quickly got her other fingers latched on, swinging her legs up to wrap around as well.

Lyrrin clung tight, squealing as though they were playing a game. She held on right around Riony's neck, little feet pushing into her hips for vantage.

"Shush!" Riony snapped, as she strained to pull them both up, balancing on the beam. "Don't you make a peep or I'll put you outside the village walls."

Drahm and Alhar walked in below them. The sparrow vulture squawked wildly, covering all other sound.

Drahm picked up a rod of steel and smacked the cage bars with it. "Shut up, bird."

The creature hissed, but backed away from the bars, quieting down.

"You didn't even let her say goodbye," Alhar said.

Riony's heart clenched. Maybe she wasn't the only one who cared. Maybe they would do something to get Kaya back.

"I hadn't intended on her going at all. You saw what happened with that big-mouthed kid!" Drahm slammed the rod back onto the anvil with a clang. "But when it came to it, we couldn't anger the dragonrider."

"Amma is very upset. She wants you to do something. Get a letter through to Kaya, maybe. That might make her stop complaining." The tone of Alhar's voice was dry, almost bored.

Riony's hopes that her supposed fiancé might fight for his sister's freedom fell away like ash. This was the tone of a man conveying a message because someone else pushed him to it.

Blight them all.

"They'll be fine, both of them. Kaya is probably living like a queen. And it was necessary."

"I don't see why. We're safe here. We've never had a problem with revs."

"That's what I thought too. But the rider knew something I didn't, about this place. About how the quarry owners left it when it was abandoned. I didn't think it could be true either, but I checked."

Drahm looked toward the closed window, face stern, then back at his son. "It is true. That's why we needed the deal."

Alhar moved closer to his father, dropping his voice. "Do we have a problem? What is it, Pabba?"

Drahm waved a hand in dismissal. "Nothing that the barrel I traded for won't fix. I've sorted it all out, I just need to arrange the right time and excuse to—"

"My arm is falling asleep," Lyrrin whispered into Riony's ear.

But she whispered it in the way a child whispers, harsh and as loud as any normal spoken voice, and Drahm and Alhar looked upward, spotting them both.

"*Lyrrin*," Riony groaned.

"Get down from there!" Drahm barked.

There was no point hiding anymore. With a sigh, Riony held Lyrrin to her side with one arm and swung down with the other, dropping down onto the blackened workshop floor.

Chest puffed out and race red with outrage, Drahm yelled, "What were you doing up there, sneaking around my forge?"

Riony straightened up, facing Drahm down with a lifted chin. "I heard what you were talking about. I heard everything."

"Did you now? Tell me, child, what did you hear?"

"That you're plotting ..." *Something. Stars. It was all too vague.* Riony tried to bluff. "That you have a secret, that you wouldn't want all the rest of the village knowing about."

A grin split Drahm's lips and he chuckled. "Are you trying to blackmail me, girl? You know nothing. What plot? What secret?"

"I know. I heard plenty," Riony didn't sound nearly as confident as she hoped. "About the ... quarry, and the barrel."

Drahm strode over to the cage with the bird in it, sliding the latch in his fingers. The bird cawed again, throwing itself wildly at the bars, eager for escape.

"What are you going to tell them? What did you hear? You'll want to be specific, or I'll let my pet out to peck out the eyes of the little one there."

Riony clutched at Lyrrin, pushing the child behind

her. "I ... I heard ... *Raze it*. I didn't hear anything."

Not enough. I didn't hear enough to mean anything!

Drahm let go of the cage latch, leaving it closed. He smiled as he marched toward the girls.

Riony backed away, pushing past Alhar who watched with raised eyebrows, and to the front door.

Drahm's smirk grew. "Run home, Riony. You've a wedding to prepare for."

Riony stumbled out backward, almost tripping on Lyrrin as the child clung to her side, pressing a hooded face to Riony. Riony and Drahm's gaze met as the door swung closed between them.

Riony fumed, eyes stinging with useless, furious frustration.

"You razing ruined my chance!" She snapped at Lyrrin. "I could have had him. I could have had ... something ... Some way to stop the marriage!"

Riony pushed Lyrrin off her. The small girl's eyes were already wet and red and she trembled.

"He wasn't really going to make his bird attack you," Riony groaned.

Was he?

"He's scary," Lyrrin whimpered. "You're being scary."

"You have no idea what scary really is!"

Lyrrin sobbed and put both hands over her face.

Riony pulled with all her inner strength on her exploding anger, drawing herself back together.

She crouched down in front of her sister, making every effort to keep her voice level and low. "Go home. Quick. And straight there this time."

Lyrrin made a pitiful whining sound, reaching gloved hands toward her sister.

Riony pushed them away, and hissed, "*Go!*"

With a sob, Lyrrin turned and ran.

Riony wiped her hands over the sting of tears in her nose and eyes and turned around toward the blacksmiths again.

She couldn't give up now. She needed *something*.

Tiptoeing to the closed door, she pressed her ear to it. Words came through as muted, hazy sounds and clipped syllables. She strained to listen.

"I don't know ... set on me marrying that thing. She's ... wild beast."

"... might tame her. But I think it might ... bad idea after all. ... trouble. Not worth keeping around. I have a better idea ... with her now."

There was a long pause. Riony shifted, ducking low to the unused keyhole, staring through then turning her ear toward it as talking began again.

Drahm's voice came through clear, slick with satisfaction. "I needed find an excuse to set off the barrel of snowflame blood. Maybe those two sisters could be the perfect scapegoats for the explosion. And unfortunate victims of it as well."

FIVE

Riony raced through the village laneways, lit by the dusky purple of the ending day. Her heart beat a raucous percussion and her head churned with the echo of Drahm's threats.

He's going to try to kill me, and Lyrrin too. We have to do something! Run away or ... Riony growled between panting breaths. *Or beat the vile creep's selfish face until he's a twin to strawberry jam.*

It took a long few moments for the ringing bell to break through and register among the churning noise in her head.

The warning muster.

"What's that tamebrain on watch doing now?" Riony muttered breathlessly as she rounded the corner to her home.

The bell had rung again only a couple of days ago—yet another false alarm. They'd become all too common.

A few windows opened, faces peering out into the gloom. Only a couple of villagers bothered a leisurely stroll to the meeting point to see what was going on.

Why rush? They had dragonrider protection now, after all.

Still aching over what that had cost, Riony pressed her teeth together so hard they hurt and she burst through her front door.

"Amma! Drahm, he's—"

"Where were you?" Eylin rounded on Riony, rolling up the wine-red sleeves of her woolen dress. "You were supposed to be here with Lyrrin while we were out. And Lyrrin tells me you were out spying? What does she mean?"

Lyrrin stood behind Eylin, clinging to their amma and watching Riony with red-rimmed eyes.

Riony turned a dark look on her little sister. "I only wanted to find out something to stop the marriage, and—"

"Farrad has gone out to find you. Pray to our ancestors

in the stars that the shadow dragon doesn't land while he's away from us." Eylin shook her head, turning back to the bag on the kitchen table and stuffing a cloth-wrapped bundle inside.

"It's not going to! Just listen."

Eylin held up a warning, shushing finger.

"Amma!"

"Go and pack!"

Grunting, Riony slammed the front door closed and stomped into her room.

She yelled over her shoulder, "Drahm wants to kill me!"

"Of course he doesn't. The marriage might feel that way, but we're not going to let—"

"No, actually kill me! He was saying things about explosives, and something about when the quarry was abandoned, and I don't know ... but he's planning something."

Riony's backpack still sat at the foot of her bed from the last warning bell, already packed badly with the head of Riony's straw doll sticking out the top. Lyrrin's doll lay on her sister's bed. Riony ignored it. The little snitch could pack her own things.

Riony went straight to her sword and hung it from

her belt. Revs or no revs, Riony knew for sure she had an enemy outside.

"Is that what you heard?" Eylin stood in the doorway.

She pulled her tangle of long red curls back and tied them in a bun. Lyrrin remained attached to her hip, hiding her face from Riony.

Shoulders drooping, Riony patted the small child on the top of her hooded head. She was rewarded with a small peek of shadowed blue eyes as Lyrrin looked to see who was touching her, and then Lyrrin swapped from her mother to Riony's side, clinging on tight.

Riony rubbed her back as a silent apology, and spoke to her mother in a low, serious tone. "The man is mad. He even threatened Lyrrin."

Eylin reached a hand to Riony, rubbing a thumb down her cheek with a sympathetic expression. "We'll work all of this out, okay? We've survived worse than that man before. We can do it again."

Riony's eyes flashed with heat and wetness and she steeled herself and nodded.

"Now, are you all packed?"

Riony pulled an annoyed face while making a show of closing her bag and throwing it over her shoulder.

The front door clattered open, and the three of them jumped.

"Pabba!" Lyrrin scolded as though he'd pulled a prank on them.

Farrad's face was drawn and pale, and when he spoke, his voice was low, husky with urgency and fear. "It's here. The shadow dragon. It's come."

Riony's mouth pulled into a lopsided smile.

He has to be joking, right? He's just trying to rile us up. Teach me a lesson for going off without Lyrrin. It can't be …

Eylin ran to the front door, turning to look toward the center of the village. She gasped, both hands covering her mouth.

Riony's smile faltered. She pushed out of Lyrrin's grip and joined her parents at the entrance to their small cottage. The three of them spilled down onto the front path, faces turned upward.

Out across the evening-soaked village, the signal tower stood in silhouette against the lilac night. Amma moon shone over them, full and round and glimmering. And then her light was cut across by a massive, looming shape.

Like black ink spilled in water, nebulous shadows roiled across the sky. The rough form of wings flapped silently.

Long dark tendrils made the shape of a whipping tail. From the creature's head, two bright points stared out. Eyes like red hot pokers glowed within the umbrous face.

The shadow dragon.

Riony's stomach dropped and her skin chilled. "What do we do?"

Eylin's head moved slowly from side to side, but her eyes remained on the descending form. "It might ... We don't know that it will land. It could move on, and there's nothing here ... it shouldn't ..."

The cursed creature, insubstantial as mist but far, far too real, descended over the center of the village. Right over the muster bell. Right over the warning signaler.

The clanging bell ceased. A few scattered screams took its place. Neighbors from all around had emerged now, watching in frozen horror.

The shadow dragon writhed, its snake-like neck thrashing as it landed, touching ground without even the whisper of noise. Then it roared.

A deep, mourning pain shot like an arrow through Riony's chest and she gasped out a sob.

What was that?

She'd never seen the shadow dragon this close before,

never had its dead-raising roar rattle through her like it was wrapping around her own bones trying to draw them to skeletal life out of her very skin.

She thought she might be scared, but the gut reaction overwhelming her was one of deep, tremendous grief.

Beside her, her parents had turned toward each other, wrapped in a sobbing embrace. A hard wallop hit Riony's side as her weeping sister collided with her, on the way to wrap her small arms around their parents.

Riony's jaw hung as the roaring stopped. She swatted away the strange tears wetting her cheeks and stared at the swirling dragon of darkness.

And at the hard stone ground beneath it.

"It's okay. Nothing's happening. Nothing is rising," she whispered like a prayer. "We're safe. We're safe here."

The solid rock of the abandoned quarry held no dead beneath them. There was nothing to answer the shadow dragon's cursed call.

Only silence followed, a few distant sounds of sobbing ... and then the cracking rumble of stone.

"What? No." Riony gasped, turning on the spot to try to locate where the sound came from.

She pushed her terrified body into action, loping a few

long strides out to the corner of the cottage so she could see down to the quarry cliff walls. To the jumble of boulders and debris piled there. Where she and the other kids played.

"Riony! Get back here!" Farrad snapped.

Riony stayed, locked in place by what she saw. The stones moved, rolling and shifting out of the way as awful, age-yellowed bones pushed from beneath. A human skull burst free in a clatter of shale, its full skeletal form stepping out after it.

Riony's trembling fingers wrapped around the hilt of her sword and her mouth went dry.

Just one. They could deal with just one revenant. Surely they could. Maybe there had been a poor soul caught under the rockslide that landed there.

Just one corpse missed in their bare village that the shadow dragon called back to ravenous life.

But the rocks kept shifting. Like a spill of marbles, the round domes of more skulls rose up from between the stones. Right where Riony and Lyrrin had jumped and played. There were so many of them, more than Riony could count with her wide, unblinking eyes. A horrific number of revenants. All human.

How are there so many of them?

Another thunderous crack of stone echoed around the village, and something even larger emerged.

A hand grabbed Riony's arm. "Back with us, come on!"

Farrad dragged her, and her feet stumbled at first, forgetting how to work as her whole body shook with fear and denial.

How were there so many dead people there? All in one place?

She turned to try to ask her father, but her words wouldn't come out.

All around them, people were moving now. Screaming to each other, running in and out of buildings.

Drahm's booming voice cut through the haunted evening. "Get to the hall! Everyone into the town hall!"

Riony's fear morphed into a burning spite.

The bodies under the rubble ... was that what he meant about this place not being safe? Did he know?

Back at their cottage, Riony's mother snatched up the bags laying half packed on their kitchen table in one arm, carrying Lyrrin in the other. "Let's go! Quick! They can bar the town hall door. We'll be safe there until help arrives. Take her, please."

Eylin leaned her hip and the child balanced on it out,

and Riony lifted her sister off and held her tight. For her own comfort as much as for Lyrrin's.

Farrad remained at the front door, watching in the direction of the rubble and the revs. Flashes moved past him in the moonlight outside as other villagers ran for shelter, the lanterns they carried streaking through the darkness.

"Faster, we have to move!" he grumbled.

"They're coming!" a woman shrieked.

"Leave it!" Farrad yelled as Eylin reached for the last bag.

Her head snapped up, and she blinked like she was waking up. Her hand went to the acorn pendant at her neck, then she nodded and they were all running, jostling against each other as they sped away from their home in a close pack.

As they ran, Riony turned her face upward. The shadow dragon was just a small spot of darkness in the already dim night, far above, blocking out the stars. The malevolent entity had done all it needed to do, laying down its curse. It moved on, leaving the dead it raised to carry out the killing for it.

To their left, a harsh cry burst from a man running near them. He toppled forward, smashing face first to the ground. His lantern smashed on the hard stone, sending bright glass shards flying as burning oil spread around.

Riony slowed on instinct, turning toward the fallen man to help him up. Then she saw why he fell.

The man's screams continued as the sickening, yellow skeleton on his back clawed through his clothing and into his flesh.

The revenant had no eyes, no brain, no organs, no flesh. But still it moved, filled with a twisted form of life and a ravenous, insatiable desire to rend humans limb from limb. Rotten teeth clacked as it gnashed at the man's neck.

His screaming cut out. Blood glistened in the dying light of the broken lantern.

Farrad grabbed Riony's arm and pulled her back into pace with him. "Keep moving!"

"What are they doing to him?" Lyrrin's voice was small in Riony's ear.

Riony's mind screamed with all the reality of what she'd just seen. One of blood and bone and painful death. Riony felt like she'd had no protection from the worst of reality for any of her own childhood.

A nasty, strange jealousy arose that Lyrrin's childhood had been so different. Part of her wanted to scream that

the man was being pulled to pieces and the same could happen to them.

She swallowed hard.

"Nothing. Don't worry. I've got you," Riony whispered back.

"Someone is at the signaler, look!" Eylin panted out the words.

The shadow dragon was no longer settled over the ground there. Its smokey form hadn't crushed anything it had landed on. It left no trace it its passing, except the undead it had raised.

The signaler still stood, no matter how the shadow dragon had writhed and raged there, as though it hated the structure.

And one brave soul was climbing it, throwing off the cloth cover, cranking the lever to angle the reflected moonlight back into the sky above.

"Get it set, now!" Drahm's voice ordered.

Will that busted thing even work at night? Riony remained skeptical. But a thin beam of blue light cut the darkness, creating a spot of bright light against the smokey clouds above them.

The town hall was a clear run in front of Riony and

her family now.

Drahm stood at the open doorway, ushering the remaining stragglers into the warm light beyond.

The man on the signaler jumped down, running up at a similar distance to Riony and her family. They were the last ones now, their cottage having been furthest away. His face came into view. Drahm's son, and Riony's supposed fiancé, Alhar.

"Come on, come on!" Drahm yelled, waving one hand at the man as he kept the other on the heavy door.

The clattering of bones against hard ground came up fast behind them.

"Alhar!" Drahm warned, taking a step away from the hall.

His son pushed himself into a faster run, but the revenants were already upon him. A pile of dozens of them rolled over him like a wave. He went down beneath them so fast he didn't even scream.

Eylin cried out wordlessly and she pushed Riony on her back, urging her faster. The shelter of the town hall was within a few strides.

Drahm moved back to the door. He turned his gaze away from where the snarling, crunching sounds came from his son's body and onto Riony and her family.

His expression darkened, and he closed the door on them, leaving them locked outside in the dark with the risen dead.

Six

Riony came up against the solid wood first, slamming into it with the shoulder that Lyrrin wasn't hanging onto.

"No! Let us in!" She kicked the door with the flat of her booted foot. "What are you doing? You can't leave us out here! You heartless creep, open the razing door!"

The door rattled but didn't give. Probably already barred on the other side. The town hall was the most secure building in the village, with thick stone walls and small, high windows. The most defensible position. The place Riony would like to be with her family. Not outside, in the dark, with revs at their back.

The few beams of golden light shining out through the cracks of the entryway and windows high above taunted Riony, a beacon of safety she couldn't reach.

"Drahm!" Farrad roared, wrenching at the door.

Murmurs and cries came through from inside. The sounds of arguments and upset. Did any of the villagers inside care about them? Care that they'd been locked out? Care enough to dare to open the door to danger again to let them in? Drahm's voice raised over the others, and the voices of dissent vanished.

What lie did he tell them to justify our deaths?

No more murmurs and cries came from inside.

Snarls and crackling bones came from behind them.

"Keep going!" Eylin reached wildly for Riony, grasping a handful of shirt at her shoulder as she pulled her family into a run again.

With a quick glance over her shoulder, Riony saw the revenants rushing down the rocky path like a boney avalanche.

With one hand on her sword hilt and the other around Lyrrin, she followed her racing parents, and then broke ahead, moving the fastest. Her backpack bounced against her shoulder blades, jostled by her sprint. The family raced around the corner of the town hall and down the side wall, keeping close as though it could hide them from the creatures chasing them.

Past the end of the hall, a cottage sat with its front door hanging open. Riony beelined for it, legs burning as she pushed herself and the extra weight she carried the fastest she'd ever run. As she burst through the entryway she spun around, hugging the wall beside the door to peer back out again.

Come on, come on!

Her parents were right behind her. Her pabba slowed slightly to push his wife through first then tumbled in after, closing the door behind him with tense precision so that it slid quietly into place.

Lyrrin squirmed in Riony's grasp. "Are we—?"

"Ssh!" Riony hissed.

No. No we're not safe, Riony's mind screamed.

Lyrrin silenced instantly, watching with worried eyes.

Riony shifted a couple of steps across to a shuttered window, pressing her eye to a small gap as she tried to control her panting breaths.

No movement outside. Nothing had followed them there. The revenants instead swarmed like ants on spilled

honey around the entrance of the town hall. The pinpricks of warm light beaming out of cracks and the hustle and murmur of packed humans inside drove the undead into a frenzy.

They yowled and clawed at the walls around the front. Riony couldn't quite see the doorway to the town hall from her angle, but could hear the *thunk, thunkthunk, thunk,* of the revenants ramming against it.

"There are so many. Where did they come from?" Eylin whispered, face pressed to a gap in the doorway.

"Under the rubble." Riony's voice was barely audible she kept it so low. "Drahm knew. I think he knew they were there. Why would so many bodies be there like that?"

Eylin and Farrad shared a tight-lipped look between them but gave no reply.

"The revs are all distracted by the people in the hall. But we still need to find somewhere safer than this." Farrad pushed a hand against the window shutters, and they wobbled loosely.

"We should run. Get to the gate and get out of here while the revs aren't paying attention to us." Riony's whole body was already tense with the desire to move, every part of her wanting to run and run and never stop to get away from the horror of the creatures outside.

"Alhar got the signaler set," Eylin said. "The dragonrider, any dragonrider, might see it, and come and clear this up. We just have to hold tight."

Riony moved back from the window. "As if. Do you really think a rider is going to come out here at night to help our little village?"

Riony's parents shared their worried look again.

Lyrrin squirmed until Riony put her down, and the small child found her own peephole to look outside. "Are the people in the hall going to be okay?"

Another round of screams reached them from the hall as the crashing grew louder.

Farrad guided Lyrrin away from the viewpoint. "I'm sure the revs won't be able to get in. It's a strong door."

"Why didn't they let us in?" Lyrrin asked.

Riony's face turned red. Drahm closed the door on them, her whole family, because of her. Because she'd dared to defend herself against him and his sick plans.

And she'd do it again. If they survived this.

But if they didn't, because of her ...

Eylin's hand found hers in the dark of the unlit cottage. "We didn't need to get into the hall. We're safe here. We'll

be safe together."

The *thunk, thunk, thunk* from the clawing revenants at the hall changed, becoming a crackling *boom, boom, boom* as something larger moved in the shadows at the end of the hall. The volume of the screaming grew to match.

Farrad looked through the gap again and cursed.

"What is it?" Riony peered out the crack near the window.

At the back of the hall, a small body was wiggling, jutting halfway out of the high back window on their belly. Golden lamp and torch light flickered all around them from inside.

"What are they doing? Why are they trying to get out?"

Farrad's face set into something grimly determined. "The revs must be getting through the front door. They're going to hurt themselves getting out of there like that."

Riony could imagine it vividly, the body toppling head-first out the narrow, high-up window, down onto the hard jumble of storage crates below.

Farrad tapped his wife on the shoulder. "Come on, we need to help them get out."

She nodded without hesitation.

Riony squeezed her mother's hand, still caught in

hers. "What? They didn't help us get *in*, why should we help them?"

"That was just Drahm. Everyone else in there is innocent," she said.

Riony scoffed.

Farrad shook his head. "They're families, like us. If you were in there, you'd want someone to help you, wouldn't you? How would you feel if nobody came?"

"I'd feel like I could look after myself! Let their precious dragonrider come save them! That's what they sold Kaya for!"

"Come on. There are still no revs around this side." Farrad pushed the door open a crack, looking ready to run out.

Eylin's hand pulled free from Riony's.

"No," Riony pleaded, sounding even younger than Lyrrin. Clearing her throat, she said firmly. "No. Safe together, remember? If you're going back out there, then so am I."

"So am I," Lyrrin echoed, coming to stand at Riony's side.

Eylin turned back from the partially opened door. She crouched down in front of the two girls, even though that

made her look up into Riony's eyes.

"I need you to listen to me right now. You need to stay here and make sure Lyrrin is safe. That's all you need to do, all I need from you, and even that is such a big responsibility I am sorry to put it on your shoulders. But I need you to keep her safe while we do this."

Eylin reached both hands to her neck and looped her thumbs under the leather string. She lifted the acorn pendant up over her head and lowered it down around Riony's.

As the acorn bumped against Riony's collarbones, Eylin cupped her cheek.

"It's a huge responsibility, but I'm asking it of you because I know you can do it. I know you're capable. I trust you, and I love you."

"Amma," was all Riony could say.

"And this," Eylin tapped on the acorn pendant and the precious treasure it held. "That's for just in case you need it, to keep yourselves alive."

"Or to come and save us with if we need it." Farrad smirked over Eylin's head. "Come on now, we have to move."

In a swish of woolen fabric and a gust of slow-cooked

meals and drying herbs scent, Riony's parents were out the door.

Lyrrin tried to run after them, and Riony snatched her back with strong arms, keeping the child beside her at the doorway as they both watched, breathlessly.

Over at the town hall, the first escapee was now hanging from their fingertips from the window ledge while two more people were trying to squeeze out the window at the same time, lanterns held out in front of them. The screaming was a non-stop howl in the background now, rising and falling in pitch as crashes and bangs carried through the night.

Below the window sat a collection of wooden crates and barrels. Riony's parents ran there, working together to lift one of the storage boxes to stack it on top of the ones closest to the wall.

The person hanging from the window dropped. They landed crookedly on the newly piled structure beneath them and tumbled sideways. Farrad caught them, turning quickly as he put them down on their feet. There was a short moment between them before the figure ran off into the dark village.

The makeshift staircase leading up to the window still

wasn't tall enough.

Eylin waved for Farrad to join her as she rolled another small barrel closer. They lifted it together, revealing the red paint around the rim.

Riony went cold all over.

Snowflame blood. Riony tried to remember exactly what that meant. Her old master knew everything about every kind of dragon species that existed. Kess would have known exactly what the little barrel could do. Riony liked thinking about Kess about as much as she liked thinking about the revenants running rampant through their village.

All Riony could think about was the word Drahm used. Explosive.

The world shook in Riony's vision, and she realized she was trembling. She turned from the work her parents were doing to Lyrrin beside her.

I have to keep her safe. But my parents ... what about them?

Those inside the hall were moving faster now there was a clear and safer escape route for them. One after another, people were rolling out the window onto the stacked containers below, being caught by Eylin and Farrad on each side as they wobbled to the ground. Clutching their lanterns and torches, they ran off like fireflies into the night.

One after another, people were saved. But their fleeing footsteps and glowing lights drew attention. From around the front of the town hall, a few skeletal revenants stalked their way.

Riony's parents were too busy to notice.

Looking again between Lyrrin and her parents, Riony clenched her teeth and grabbed Lyrrin's hand. A second later they were running. Not fast enough. Riony ducked back to scoop Lyrrin up, barreling across the ground toward her parents. Her backpack bounced against her back and sword swung at her side.

"They're coming. We have to go, the revs are coming!" Riony called out in a raspy voice, too scared to yell loudly in case she drew the undead straight to her and Lyrrin.

Her warning was lost beneath all the other voices.

The screaming hit a fever pitch as the walls of the town hall shook from within. Something big was moving around in there. Something was making awful, crunching, tearing noises in there.

In the mad rush to escape, an older man fell out the window in a wild summersault. His glass lantern clattered from his hand, flying upward briefly before smashing down onto the makeshift staircase. The oil spread quickly, lighting up the wood of the barrels, burning on the red-rimmed barrel.

Snowflame blood. Explosive.

"Run, RUN!! Riony screamed as she raced for her parents.

They heard her then, turning away from the catching fire and escaping villagers. Taking in the approaching revenants. Eyes turning to their daughters, full of concern.

There was a pop, and a soft sizzling sound as the red-rimmed barrel split, and then with the boom of close-lightning, the world exploded.

SEVEN

A wall of heat rushed over Riony. She crouched low, holding Lyrrin close, bending over her sister as sparks and spitting flames rained over them.

Darkness thickened the air and Riony coughed as her throat filled with acrid gas.

She blinked stinging eyes, worried the blast had sent her blind. Then the air gusted, moving the thick, black smoke in a swirl of cinders.

Coughing again, Riony yelled, "Amma! Pabba?"

"Where are they?" Lyrrin's voice was muffled within Riony's tight hold.

"They're ..."

They were right near the revs. Right near the explosion.

No. They were moving away from it. I warned them. They can't be ...

"They're nearby."

Getting back to her feet, Riony moved in a sightless stumble in the direction she thought her parents had been. There were groans and cries all around, some cut off short by the snarling gnash of teeth.

Other people. Not my parents. Not them.

The thought did little to comfort Riony. Every person in pain, every person becoming a victim to the revenants was someone she knew. Friends and playmates and neighbors and they were all screaming and dying.

A hot ember stuck on Riony's cheek, and she hissed. Her frantic movements made Lyrrin's hood fall down, and she pulled it back over her sister's head, protecting her from the swirling, stinging heat.

The smoke churned as someone raced past in front of her, panting and sobbing. There was a flash of blue clothing—not her parents.

"Amma?" Riony rasped out a desperate cry.

"Riony!" Farrad's voice cut through the haze, sounding

distant.

"Where are you?" Eylin's voice followed.

Riony choked on relief. She hurried toward her parents' voices.

Her feet hit something heavy and soft, catching before she could avoid tripping. Momentum tipped her forward. She arched back, pulling Lyrrin and her face away from the rapidly approaching ground and hit hard on her knees instead. One made a nasty cracking sound against the stone ground.

Pain crumpled Riony and she fell to one side.

"Ow," Lyrrin grumbled, wriggling to free herself from Riony's awkward, sideways hold.

"Riony?" Her mother's voice sounded farther away.

Riony opened her mouth to call back, but as the smoke gusted and cleared, she saw what she'd stumbled on. Jorrick, laying face up, eyes open and lifeless. There were no marks on him, no clawed gouges or bite marks from the attacking skeletons.

A chunk of charred stone lay beside him, and blood pooled around the back of his head.

As more screams pierced the lifting smoke, Riony stared at him numbly, wondering if maybe he'd gotten

lucky with such a quick, clean death.

The air became clearer, and red light filtered through from all around, flickering and warm. The crackle of fire lifted Riony's gaze away from the lifeless body of her friend. *Friend.* Dumb, tamebrain bully, but someone she had known and played with since coming to the village.

We could all be dead soon. We will be for sure if you don't get up and do something!

Closing her eyes and breathing out the pain in her knees, Riony moved into a sitting position, preparing to get back to her feet.

Lyrrin screamed, short and high pitched. She pulled entirely free from Riony and hid behind her, giving Riony a clear view of the reason the child had cried out.

Through the dark smoke, a yellowed skeleton clawed at Jorrick's legs, shaking the body as though checking for signs of life. A hiss came from its toothy skull despite having no throat, no lungs to pump air. It swiveled its head as though looking, searching, despite having no eyes.

Riony held her own breath, edging away from the monster. It hadn't come after Lyrrin for screaming, but there were still screams all around. Maybe it thought the cry came from Jorrick.

But it was close. Too close, and on its endless quest to find human life and snuff it out.

Riony grasped for the hilt of her sword. The action made the blade scrape on the ground, and the rev's head pivoted toward her.

With a gasp, Riony drew her sword in a swinging block in front of her as the undead creature flung itself her way. Lyrrin screamed again.

The blade caught on the side of the revenant's skull, chipping bone. Its head wobbled on bare spine bones then it launched itself at Riony again.

Crab walking backward, Riony swung again wildly, cutting between the ribs and collarbones, sending a spindly piece of yellowed matter flying free. The revenant didn't slow down. One of its arms struck out, scraping down Riony's cheek. She roared out in primal rage and pain as sharp fingerbones cut her flesh under her eye.

She put her sword up between them again, but down on the ground she had no good angle, no leverage, no reach, and no training to know how to use any of those things even if she had them. All she could do was swipe the weapon in front of her, chipping away at the monster who would never stop coming after them.

The bloodied claws of the revenant reached for Riony again, going for her eyes. Then it was pulled back, wrenched from Riony's view.

Breath caught in her throat, Riony searched for the threat, seeing the revenant lifted up bodily, the entire skeleton held up by neck and hipbone above her father's head.

With both strong arms, Farrad threw the rev hard into a nearby wall. Osseous matter smashed from the point of impact, and the revenant fell in a crumple of twisted and still twitching bones.

"Pabba!" Lyrrin ran for him first, tangling herself up in his legs.

Eylin appeared through the smoke beside him, scooping up the child. "My Lil Moon."

Farrad stepped forward, limping. The entire left side of his face was bloody, but he smiled as he bent down to help Riony to her feet.

Riony winced as she put weight on her aching knees but suppressed it. Her parents had asked her to be strong, to be responsible, and she had. She'd kept Lyrrin safe, and they were back together, and she'd keep being strong until they were all safe.

Eylin moved closer, hugging Riony in a way that pressed Lyrrin between them. "My girls."

"Come on," Farrad stepped in behind them, gently pushing them into motion.

It took Riony a couple of hesitant steps to be sure she could walk without falling, and then they were all running together.

Riony wiped her smoke ravaged eyes, trying to make sense of what she was seeing. She seemed to be right at the back of the town hall now, but the shape of the building was all wrong.

Cracked stones lay all around them, the remnants of what was the back wall. All the crates and barrels were now splinters. There were more bodies.

Drahm was going to do this to Lyrrin and me.

Riony's teeth clenched. If she hadn't listened in, found out what he was up to with that barrel of snowflame blood, she could have been one of those bodies. Her parents would have been among those bodies.

Seeing the scale of the destruction, Riony wondered if it would have been enough to clear the bones from under the rockfall they'd crawled out of. That must have been what Drahm wanted it for. Blast all those hidden bodies away before this exact event happened.

He was too late. And Riony doubted it would have worked anyway. It knocked down one wall of the town hall, but mostly, the snowflame blood just burned.

The flying splatters of burning liquid had hit the thatched cottage roofs all around, and half the village was catching alight.

Less of the thick black smoke from the blast hung in the air now, but the drifting gusts from the smaller fires were taking its place.

Riony's fingers clenched around the hilt of her sword, the dragonscale pattern biting into her skin. She and her parents had run together, just like this, after they'd taken Lyrrin. The same sword stuck in Riony's rigid grasp, unwilling to let go of the reassurance the weapon gave her.

Her family moved fast, and as much as Riony tried to keep up, she fell behind. She tried to push through the pain in her knees, but her body wouldn't physically let her bend them enough to run her normal speed. She hobbled unevenly after her parents as they headed toward the village gates.

They needed to get out. It was now safer outside the protection of their village walls than it was inside it. They

were fish in a barrel.

A wide mouthed, hollow-eyes skull appeared from the smoke at Riony's side, snapping at her. She smacked the pommel of her sword into it with a wide punch, sending it spinning back into the smoke it had emerged from.

Another more human cry came from up ahead, and the pound of footsteps on stone echoed all around, matching the beat of Riony's heartbeat thudding in her ears and her rapid, panting breath.

From the middle of the village, the weak beam of moonlight reflected by the signaler still shone up into the sky above. But no dragonrider came to save them. The rising smoke drifted through the beam, smothering even the hope the signal might reach help.

Up the road, lamp-light streaked across the darkness, then smashed down to the ground, followed by a scream.

Eylin and Farrad skidded to a stop, hesitating long enough for Riony to catch up.

"I see three of them," Eylin whispered.

Riony squinted into the dark, her eyes blurry from the smoke. "We can make a break for it, go around them."

"We're not fast enough." Eylin's gaze flickered down to Riony's legs, her husband's limp, then she pulled Lyrrin

in closer, patting her back and making hushing sounds.

"I can make it," Riony said.

Farrad took a couple of steps back to look around the corner of the nearest building. "Raze it. In here, quick!"

The click-clack of old bones jarring against each other approached fast from behind them.

Farrad held open the door to Drahm's blacksmith forge, and Eylin carried Lyrrin in, with Riony and Farrad close behind.

He slammed the door closed and pushed against it as fleshless bodies hit it from the other side. He growled as he put all his weight into holding it closed. Riony joined him, pushing her shoulder into the wood.

Claws rattled the door, swiping again, then again, and then quieted.

Farrad slumped into a quiet sigh, bending as he continued leaning on the door. He whispered, "I think they've moved on."

Eylin put Lyrrin down in the middle of the room, then slid a heavy barrel across the floor.

"We can't stay in here forever." Riony moved out of the way, helping her mother barricade the door with the barrel.

"We can stay until it's safe."

"When will it be safe? Do you think the revs are just going to give up and leave? There's no where for them to go! We should have run, back before the explosion. We should have run and been gone, out the gates, safe together." Riony's voice rose above a whisper, and a growl came through the door.

She backed away from it, turning around on the spot. The couple of windows were shuttered and barred already. She turned once, twice, as though her searching eyes could find the solution to save her family.

She was halted from her frantic spinning by her mother's gentle hands. They cupped her cheek.

"We had to help the others, and it was worth it. It's always worth trying to help." Eylin's voice was both soft and firm, as her eyes lingered on Riony's other cheek, dripping blood from her wound. "And if we're lucky, someone will come and help us too. We'll get out of this."

They stood together in silence, waiting, but nobody came.

There were only screams outside.

The only light in the smithy was the low glow of coals cooling in the forge. In the corner, feathers rustled. Beady eyes opened, shining from the dark corner, woken by the commotion.

The eyes locked onto Riony and her family, and the sparrow-vulture squawked harshly.

"Shush, bird, quiet!" Farrad stepped beside the cage, making calming gestures.

The bird cawed even louder, snapping at him through gaps in the cage.

The barred windows rattled and crashed. The door shook. Growls reverberated in as the revenants threw themselves at the wood blocking them from their prey, riled up by the screeching bird.

Timber cracked as hinges split from their frame. Farrad rushed beside the wobbling shutters, trying to hold them closed. Eylin pulled Lyrrin to her side and turned around the way Riony had, seeking shelter.

"Up! We have to go up." Riony tucked her sword through her belt and pointed to the high rafters above them.

Eylin nodded, lifted Lyrrin, and placed her onto Riony's back. "Quick."

Lyrrin grabbed on tight as Riony led the way, taking a wobbling step up on a barrel then jumping for the rafter. She barely caught it, her fingertips slipping then catching at the last moment. Straining with effort, Riony pulled

herself and Lyrrin up onto the beam.

From the doorway, wood cracked and split with another wall shaking rattle.

Eylin tried to follow after Riony, but her jump didn't reach. She landed back on the ground again with a gasp. Farrad rushed to her side, holding her around the waist and lifting her up over his shoulders.

Riony twisted around onto her stomach, reaching back in return. Her mother's fingertips brushed against hers ...

Then jerked away, as revenants flooded into the room, crashing into Farrad and knocking both of Riony's parents down.

EIGHT

The scarlet-lit room below Riony became a sea of hideous, clacking bones, and yellowed teeth and claws. Swirling, thrashing, snarling.

A scream stuck in Riony's throat, her whole body rigid with fear. The tips of her fingers tingled where her mother's had slipped through hers. Her hand closed reflexively into a tight fist, as though doing so could take her back in time to catch the other hand in hers.

"Amma?" Blinking stinging eyes, Riony tried to track her parents in the fray.

With a sharp crack, the bulb of one rev's skull exploded into shards. Farrad stood behind it, mid-swing with a long-handled mallet. Another skeletal form clung onto his back, teeth pressing into the meat of his shoulder. Blood dripped.

"Pabba!"

He swung again, arcing through another revenant's rib cage, sending it staggering.

At his side, Eylin cried out, a sound of unbearable pain. Then words followed, still sounding like a scream. "Stay up there! Keep her safe!"

Riony thrust her hand down again, reaching for her parents. "Jump! I'll catch you."

The bodies below, both alive and undead, churned in a messy melee. Eylin had a pair of heavy pliers gripped in both hands. She swung and snapped them at the fleshless human forms. But there was no fear, no hesitation in the creatures. Only bloodlust. Only a curse-driven desire to tear living flesh apart.

"Come on!" Riony squealed, high and desperate, reaching her arm down so fiercely she could have popped her shoulder from its socket.

Farrad disappeared beneath a mountain of writhing bones.

The sparrow-vulture in its cage screeched, piercing

above all the other sound, as the heavy scent of blood and worse filled the room. Driven into as much of a frenzy as the undead, the bird raged against the bars.

With a scream that could have cut Riony in two, Eylin fell beneath the revenants as well.

"What are they doing? What are the bones doing to Amma and Pabba?" Lyrrin's question stuttered out through tears.

Breathing through her own wracking sobs, Riony twisted around on the rafters until she was more upright, with her back against a vertical beam. The soft contents of her backpack squashed between her and the thick wood. She pulled Lyrrin in close.

Her hand ached with the desire to reach for her sword, to go down and fight.

But even her father, tall and strong, hadn't been able to slow the creatures down.

Even her mother, clever and brave, hadn't been able to escape.

"Nothing. Shh, shh." Riony placed her hands around Lyrrin, covering her ears and eyes as tightly as she could.

So that Lyrrin couldn't hear the chewing, the gurgling gasps, the slow *shhhllrp* of tearing flesh. So Lyrrin couldn't see their mother's blank eyes, staring up from where she lay on the floor, body shaking and twitching as revs ripped into her from all sides.

Lyrrin couldn't see the blood spattering. Pooling. Lyrrin couldn't hear it when her parents stopped screaming. Stopped breathing.

I could still do something. Still save them. There has to be something ...

Riony had her sword, and she had the silvernix. If she could get down there, she could revive them with the magical unicorn blood.

But her hands were locked around Lyrrin and her head was filled with visions of what might happen to the child if Riony went down there ... and then didn't come back.

The acorn pendant that hid the precious glass vial within hung like a weight around Riony's neck. The promise of salvation.

But there was no way to safely reach her parents to use it. The revenants remained, swarming over their victims.

Farrad had gone quiet and still. Eylin kept twitching. *Pabba. Amma.*

The revenants continued their butcher's work.

The bird kept squawking.

Riony couldn't think over all the sounds and sights so horrific she could barely comprehend them beyond how they made her own living bones feel cold as ice.

She wished she could cover her own eyes and ears.

But she waited, and she watched, and she clung desperately to hope.

If Lyrrin and I can just stay quiet enough so the revs don't find us, if the revs just leave to find someone else, or if someone else comes to help us, then I can go down to Amma and Pabba and save them with the silvernix.

Save *them?* Both? Riony wasn't sure if the dose of silvernix was enough for two people. It was a single drop.

What if I have to choose? How could I choose?

She didn't know enough about it, how to use it, whether it would be enough to heal the wreckage of even one of the bodies below. Whether they were already too far gone.

Riony knocked the back of her head against the beam behind her, pressing her eyes closed against the flow of tears. She didn't know what to do. Lyrrin trembled in her arms and her parents were dying, dying ... *dead?* ... and she couldn't *do anything.*

Nobody came.

Nobody came to save them.

Maybe everyone else was already dead.

Maybe it would have been better if they had all died together.

Riony grew still, her body a war of burning, strained muscles and chilled, roiling insides. The only movement was the flow of tears down her cheeks.

There were no sounds of life from her parents anymore. It had been a while now. Too long. Despite Riony's most desperate hopes, she knew it had been too long.

There was no way to save them now.

But the revenants wouldn't leave. Her mother's body kept twitching—Riony had seen it before when processing chickens. Sometimes muscles didn't know the rest of the body was dead and kept moving long afterward.

The movement kept driving the creatures into a frenzy. They had no interest in the caged bird beside them, as monstrous as them as it tried to break free and feast on the spread of meat before it. The revs only cared about making the human stop moving.

It seemed to take forever. Riony stayed there, painfully perched on that beam, holding her sister and humming soft notes of a lullaby. She stayed as all the sweat from their earlier chase chilled on her skin, and the air filled with smoke.

Her heart ached like a weight in her chest for all she'd just lost.

Amma. Pabba.

She stayed there, waiting for her and Lyrrin to be the next to die.

Would it be the same? Twitching in agony on the floor for so, so long?

Stars, please, please stop moving.

Riony couldn't take any more. She could only wish for it all to be over. She wanted all of the pain and horror to end. She was ready to go into the stars with her parents and all family they had lost before.

But the twitching and gnawing and scrabble of boney claws pulling free all the soft parts of what was her mother went on forever. Until Riony had forgotten how to breathe from holding in her screams. Until she had turned to stone, locked in her protective hold around Lyrrin.

Lyrrin.

Their Little Moon. The precious child Riony had stolen as a baby to keep her alive.

Riony was all Lyrrin had now. And Lyrrin all she had in return.

Imagining for Lyrrin the fate her parents had suffered struck Riony like a red-hot poker, igniting her insides. Kindling her will to stay alive. For her.

"I'm going to keep you safe. I'm going to get you out of this," Riony whispered so low she could barely hear her own words over the cacophony below.

But the promise rung loud inside her. They were going to survive this.

Riony should have known no one would come to save them.

Nobody had ever come to save her. Not when she'd been tied to the Heithorn whipping post. Not when the command was giving that her and her mother and a newborn baby were to be killed.

She'd only ever survived because she'd saved herself. And she was determined to do it again.

Except Riony didn't know how. The only way out was past the bodies of her parents below, and the revs still hanging over them, flies clinging to corpses.

The undead hadn't spotted the sisters yet. They were safe in the rafters, but if they climbed down there was no way to get past the revenants without being seen and they would die just the same as their parents had.

Riony coughed, the air clouding as smoke thickened. She could barely see anymore.

From below there was the clang of metal, a different sound amongst the clack of bones. Riony's heartrate spiked, hoping to see the swing of weapons, someone coming to save them. She squinted down through the drifting smoke.

In the corner, the birdcage lay on its side.

Through the haze, the sparrow-vulture appeared in a burst.

Its hooked beak went straight for Riony's eyes. Tensing, Riony clamped her mouth closed against a cry and threw one arm up in defense.

The motion sent Riony sideways, teetering on the edge of the beam. She dropped her legs, squeezing her thighs around the wood to steady herself and Lyrrin.

Tattered feathers beat the air around her. The bird squawked and scratched at Riony's arms as she fought to keep the vulture from reaching her face, or Lyrrin.

Talons pierced through Riony's bare wrists and palms, cutting red ribbons.

Get off me! Go away, you blighted creature! Riony screamed in her head, teeth still gritted in her attempt to stay quiet and hidden.

The bird hovered, flapping back and forth around Riony as it harried her. Her attempts to swat it away only seemed to enrage it more. Free from its cage, it gleefully took out vengeance for its captivity on the first human it found.

Riony bit back another cry as its beak snapped around her ear.

With one hand around Lyrrin, she reached back with the other, grasping around the upright beam behind her for purchase. Bringing one foot up, she kicked out at the sparrow-vulture.

Her boot connected with the bird's breastbone, sending it backward in a flurry of feathers and screeches. It hit another beam, fell, righted itself, and spotted the broken front door.

With one final, insulted caw, it fled out into the night.

Riony closed her eyes to the pain it had left marked across her arms and face. Warn liquid trickled down her neck. She took a deep, relieved breath.

And then rough, hard fingers closed on the toes of her leg that was dangling down astride the beam.

With a scream, Riony looked down. A mass of dark-eyed skulls stared back. Arms reached high, swaying like reeds beside a river. Reaching for Riony, and Lyrrin.

Riony wrenched her leg up, tugging at the grasp of the one tallest rev who had grabbed her foot. It held tight. Roaring with effort, Riony pulled upward, wriggling and twisting her ankle to pull free. Her boot slipped off, still in the rev's hands, and she brought her leg out of reach as fast as she could.

But all of the revs had seen them now. And they were doing everything they could to reach them.

The skeletons piled atop one another in their effort to catch their prey. A small mountain of bones, lifting each other up from the sheer mass of them more than any kind of conscious co-operation. Their boney fingers scraped the rafter Riony balanced on.

Riony got her bare foot under her, crouching on the beam.

"Hold on. Hold tight!" Riony ordered Lyrrin.

Lyrrin made no sound in return, but her arms and legs latched on around Riony. Her face pressed into Riony's chest, making her shirt there wet.

Riony rose to her feet, using both arms to lift the two of them up onto a higher diagonal rafter. Out of reach, but not for long.

The air was thick with smoke now.

Coming in from outside? Or ...?

Riony turned her gaze toward the thatched roof above. Glittering spots of red shone down through the haze. The fire from the explosion had spread. The roof was burning.

The thick thatching only smoldered so far, but once it caught, Riony and Lyrrin would burn too from the heat above them.

And below, the revenants kept climbing.

Nine

Riony's lungs burned, and her eyes streamed with tears from the sting of smoke. She could barely see as she searched for some way to escape the threats from both above and below.

Skeletal fingers scratched at her toes, and she blindly grasped for the next rafter above her. There wasn't much higher she could climb. The ceiling was right above them, the thatching hot and crackling with flames. Riony had to crouch to avoid scrapping her head on the rough ceiling.

A boney hand swiped through the smoke and Riony jerked away from it, pulling her clinging sister closer. Lyrrin squealed.

How am I going to get us out of here?

Below was a swirl of motion and clacking bones. Above, fire burned through the roof.

Through the thatching.

Heartbeat racing, Riony sought out the brightest glow of red in her blurred vision. Her cheeks heated as she moved toward the closest, balancing step-by-step in a strained crouch along the beam, Lyrrin hanging heavy on her front and her pack on her back.

Undamaged thatching would be way too hard to break through, but where the flames turned sections of the thick, bundled straw to embers, Riony might be able to get free.

Holding a beam for balance, Riony balled her other hand into a fist and punched it toward the burning ceiling.

Scalding pain burst across her knuckles as she made contact. Ashes rained down over her and Lyrrin, and she made sure Lyrrin's hood was up, covering her head. Riony shook out her burned hand.

Stars. This is going to hurt.

But Riony was no stranger to pain. It wouldn't hurt more than the whippings she'd once endured as a child. It wouldn't hurt more than the loss scalding her heart. She could do this.

The snarl of revs closing in through the smoke meant she had to.

With a loud grunt, Riony punched at the ceiling again. She felt the give of the crumbling, searing straw. One more hit, and her fist pushed right through. Flames flickered all around the hole, catching faster now the thatching had been thinned.

Riony's fingers and wrist burned from the touch of those flames, and the hole was still too small.

"There's one behind you!" Lyrrin half-screamed, holding Riony tighter.

Riony didn't take time to confirm her sister's warning. She could hear the bones clacking over the beam she stood on. She instead placed herself directly under the burning hole, bent forward in her crouch. Then she pushed her back upward with all her strength.

Her backpack gave her some protection from the first contact with the fire, but embers scattered all across her arms and head as she pressed upward. The small hole she'd punched through split, growing wider. Roaring with effort, Riony pushed with all the strength she had. Burned straw snapped and tore.

The crackle of fire and ripping of straw and thud of

her own heartbeat and screams of her sister and snarling of the rev filled her ears and then with one final push, Riony burst free into the cool nighttime air above the building.

She gasped a deep breath into aching lungs. She didn't slow down, pulling Lyrrin up through the hole next then leaning back on the surrounding, burning roof to leverage her legs up after them.

Her bare foot caught on the flaming edges and Riony hissed, trying to roll clear, but the backpack and child and sword at her hip made the motion too difficult and instead sent all of them sliding down the pitched roof.

"Woah, woah, woah!" Riony twisted, trying to slow their fall.

They went over the edge of the high roof. Riony caught the eave with her burned hand, crying out at the agony of holding all their weight with her blistered skin. Her fingers slipped. With her other arm around Lyrrin, they dropped again.

She'd slowed their fall enough, and they landed upright, Riony's sore knee flaring up and sending stars into her vision.

Every part of Riony felt torn and charred and broken. With a grunt, she brought her and Lyrrin back up to

standing.

They were at the back of the blacksmiths. She just had to head straight, reach the palisades, then right to the gates and be away from the revs and out of this nightmare.

Without Amma and Pabba.

That was a nightmare Riony couldn't escape.

The smoke had lifted, filling the sky above them as a soft breeze cleared the ground.

Riony wanted to run, but the best she could manage was a slow hobble.

Tears flowed uncontrollably down her cheeks, silently, from both the smoke and her bone-deep grief. Cottage walls of stone and raised garden beds of rice and flowers passed by in the darkness, lit orange by the flames topping almost every building. There was a scream in the distance. The splash of water down at the reservoir.

Lyrrin lifted her head, mumbling something Riony couldn't make out.

Riony kept both arms wrapped around her sister. "Shh. We're going to be safe soon."

Riony's heart hurt. They could get out of the gates, no longer penned in with death all around, but outside their village walls was far from safe.

But she would keep moving, keep trying, keep fighting to keep them both alive.

The gates were within sight. As Riony moved passed the final cottage, a figure shifted in the shadows.

It stepped out, looming in front of Riony. She grasped the hilt of her sword, ready to either run or fight.

"Where are you going?" Drahm's voice was wild and scratchy. Blood dripped down one side of his face and his eyes were wide. He carried a long sword in one hand, blade chipped and charred with soot.

Riony's lips twisted in a snarl, but she didn't give the man a reply. She tried to keep moving around him.

His gaze turned between Riony and the gates she headed toward. "You're trying to leave?"

He snatched for Riony. She dodged away.

"Yes, we're leaving!" Riony growled back. "Why would we stay here? Everything here is dead. Everyone is ..."

Her voice broke over the final word.

Drahm waved a heavy arm through the air dismissively. "Many of the revenants were destroyed in the explosion. We just need to hold on a bit longer until the dragonriders come."

Riony barked a high, hysterical laugh. "You think

someone's coming to save you? Nobody is coming!"

Drahm stalked closer. "They will, we've signaled them."

Riony backed away, circling, trying to get closer to the gate. "And why do you think that signaler the rider brought you was burned when you got it? Because they don't come, they don't help. The place he got it from didn't need it anymore because everyone there was probably dead. Just like everyone here."

"No! We'll be safe here, soon. We all have to stay. We need everyone to rebuild again." Drahm jabbed his sword in the air, punctuating his words.

"Even people you were ready to kill? I know you were going to use that explosive barrel on us." Riony bent forward, putting Lyrrin down on her feet.

"Get ready to run," she whispered before straightening up again.

Once her sister was standing, she pushed the child around behind her.

Chin lifted, Riony growled. "You knew, didn't you? You knew all those bodies were under the rubble."

"It was only rumors ... until Veyrn confirmed." Drahm's expression twisted, something almost like guilt, but he shook it off fast. "The quarry wasn't profitable, and the owners didn't want the expense of transporting their resources when they closed down. So they disposed of them all there."

"Resources? They were people!" Riony's nose scrunched with the sting of fury.

All those people, slaves, put to work for the dragonlords who owned the quarry, and then killed and buried on site when they were no longer needed, like they were worth nothing. Riony couldn't comprehend the cruelty.

But it didn't surprise her.

"And you lied!" she snapped at Drahm and drew her own sword. "You said we were safe here, at the same time as selling off Kaya and ruining us all with your deal!"

She jabbed her sword, pointing it toward the devastation in the center of their village.

There were fewer screams now. Many must have died in the explosion. And anyone left was being picked off by the remaining revs.

Drahm's neck and shoulders stiffened visibly. Any regret or guilt overcome as his commanding tone returned. "It wasn't my fault the shadow dragon came! I had everything worked out! If we'd just had more time, everything would have been fine."

"And you count killing me and my sister as being fine? If you had time to follow your plans, we'd be dead. And if we stay here, we'll all be dead."

Drahm reached both hands for her in a gentle gesture. "You don't have to be! We need every body we can to rebuild our community. I only ever wanted what is best for all of us. You can trust me."

Riony laughed, dark and low. "Tell that to Kaya."

"I had to make some hard decisions, but that's what a leader does. And it was worth it! We used the signaler. A rider will come!"

Riony let her words out slowly. "Dragonriders can't be trusted. Anyone who would sell their daughter into slavery can't be trusted. When you only see other people's lives as something you can use and spend, one day, all of that debt will catch up to you."

With her burned hand, Riony gave Lyrrin a shove away from her, hoping the child would take the hint and run.

Then she stepped forward and took her best swing at Drahm.

Her blow was blocked by a swift motion of his sword, the impact jarring through Riony's wrist.

Riony cursed, gritting her teeth. She'd never been in a

sword fight before. She'd hoped for the element of surprise, to hit Drahm and get him out of her way before he could fight back. But his eyes widened with a feral fury at her attempt and he struck back.

Drahm swung hard and fast, blow after blow that Riony wasn't prepared to match. She stumbled backward and ran into the small body of her sister, hesitating behind her.

"Raze it!" Riony grasped at Lyrrin, keeping them both from falling as she ducked under another swing.

Drahm's arms, thick and strong from blacksmithing, looked like they could easily crush her with any one of his blows.

The village leader's longsword glinted in the firelight as he brought it up overhead then crashing down.

Riony pushed Lyrrin off to the left as she fell to the right, the sword slicing down where they'd just been.

Agony smashed through Riony as she hit the hard ground. The back of her head bounced on the stone. Her vision dimmed and everything hurt. Inside and out, all she knew was pain.

Drahm stood over her, leisurely lining up his blade with her heaving chest.

He was too strong, and Riony too unskilled with her sword. She'd been a fool trying to fight him.

Drahm glared down the length of his sword at her. "You really are too much trouble to keep. Better I get rid of you now. At least I'll still have the younger one."

"No cursed way will you have her," Riony spat back.

She pushed his sword away with hers and rolled back to her feet. Pure spite and desperation flooded through her, keeping her battered body moving. But her vision swam and she couldn't win this fight through spite and grit alone.

Then the smoke behind Drahm swirled, moving in the low light.

And Riony smirked, lowering her sword. "Maybe you were right after all."

Drahm hesitated on his next swing, confusion twisting his brow. "About what?"

Riony flicked her chin to point behind him. "Look. Here comes your dragon to save you now."

With a skeptical expression, the man half turned to peer over his shoulder.

The shape of a dragon moved toward them, silhouetted by the fire behind it.

Drahm huffed in relief, turning fully toward the

approaching shape. "You've come! You've come to save us!"

Riony's smirk dropped, only pain and sadness inside her now. It almost hurt to hear the hope and triumph in Drahm's voice. Riony almost wished it was true.

But she knew the dragonriders would never come.

With Drahm's back to her, distracted by what he believed was his salvation, she could finish him then and there. Get revenge for Kaya, for all his threats, for all he put her and her family through.

But none of that felt important anymore. Only one thing was. Riony grasped to her side, finding Lyrrin there.

And the approaching dragon shape sped up, growling and snarling.

"What? What is this?" Drahm remained on the spot, staring, unbelieving.

The dragon's head came into view. Rotten scales hung on an eyeless skull. Human slaves weren't the only resource the quarry owners must have disposed of under that landslide.

The revenant dragon lunged and was upon Drahm in a flash.

Riony scooped Lyrrin into her arms and used all the strength she had remaining to run.

TEN

Bodies trudged, zombie-like all around Riony.

Refugees. All lost and broken and hurt in ways that might never heal. But surviving. Like Riony and Lyrrin.

They had found each other along the way, all heading to the same destination. They stuck together for safety.

Their numbers had been greater before. More had been lost along the way, because there was no real safety to be found in a land at war between revenants and dragonriders.

After a while, they no longer made an effort to learn each other's names, to ask how they had come to be where they were.

Everyone was exhausted, frayed thin from their long journey.

Now their destination was close. It had to be. They'd run out of food two days ago and the rocky mountain track provided nothing to sustain them.

"Almost there," Riony said to herself as much as anyone else.

Please let it be real. Please let it be close.

All those travelling with them had heard the rumors of the safe city underground in the mountains. None of them knew for sure. They all hoped they were going the right way.

The straw feet of a doll danced on Riony's head and Lyrrin hummed a soft tune from above where she rode on Riony's shoulders. Her breath wafted down over Riony, minty from the herb leaf Riony had given her to suck on to relieve her hunger. Her last one.

Cold air blew down from the snowy peaks far above, and Riony folded her arms over Lyrrin's dangling legs in an attempt to stay warm. She felt so tired.

"Almost there," she repeated again, barely a whisper.

"You said almost there yesterday. And the day before."

"And you said you were a big strong person who didn't

need piggy backs yesterday and the day before, and yet here we are."

Lyrrin didn't offer a reply, just kept dancing the doll on Riony's head.

Then she sighed. "Are Amma and Pabba going to be there? When will they be back?"

Riony stiffened, swallowed, and took a deep breath. "They're not coming back, Lyrrin. Amma and Pabba are gone forever."

"Stop saying that!" The straw doll came flying down, thrown into the dirt.

Riony had explained before. Over and over. She'd tried her best, as gently as she could, to make Lyrrin understand.

"I'm so sorry, Lil Moon. I'm sorry I couldn't save them."

"Don't call me that!" Lyrrin screeched. "Put me down. PUT ME DOWN!"

Riony crouched down and her sister slid off her back. The child picked up a rock in each gloved hand and threw them off the mountainside. Eyes wet and cheeks red, she stomped over to the thrown doll and picked it up roughly, sobbed once, and then pulled the doll into a tight embrace.

It had been like that ever since they left the village. Ever since that night.

Ever since ...

Lyrrin woke up screaming most nights.

Before, she'd been a good kid. Occasionally petulant, but generally quiet and obedient.

Now, she snapped at everything and made a point of being contrary. Tears came easily and often.

Riony had tried her hardest to hide the worst of what happened from Lyrrin's eyes, but she was worried about how much Lyrrin heard and saw. How it had changed her.

How it changed them both.

"Come here, lil ... little spitfire." Riony remained crouched, opening her arms wide.

Lyrrin rushed into them and Riony held her close.

Lyrrin whispered, "I'm sorry."

The other refugees kept moving around them without a glance down.

From the front of the group came a cry. Riony tensed, reaching for her sword.

And then there was the ripple of applause and happiness.

"There it is! There's the entrance!" Someone yelled back.

A real smile split Riony's lips for the first time in a long time. "You hear that? It's up ahead! We'll be there soon."

We'll be safe soon.

Lyrrin pulled out of her hold, bright blue eyes still red, but no longer crying.

The red ribbon around the straw doll was dusty, and Riony reached over the brush it off. Lyrrin snatched it away.

"Stop it. She's mine!"

Riony frowned slightly. She wasn't sure whether Lyrrin had simply claimed Riony's red-ribboned doll because the blue one had been left behind, or whether Lyrrin really couldn't remember that one wasn't really hers.

Lyrrin's memory of everything that happened before had also become patchy. Riony only hoped it helped the child forget the worst of what they'd been through, and what they'd lost. She didn't correct Lyrrin about the doll.

"Come on. I want to be one of the first people inside!" Riony grabbed Lyrrin's hand, and they picked up their pace to push through to the front of the crowd.

The rubbly goat track flattened out ahead of them into a plateau, with a perpendicular cliff shooting upward on one side.

Built into that cliff were two massive stone doors.

It's real. Riony inhaled sharply as she took in the solid entrance. The thick stone looked impenetrable, ancient,

and magical.

The doors were carved from limestone streaked with sparkling crystal. The intricate relief that had been sculpted into the stone showed a beautiful scene of elegant trees, twining together into knotwork. Between the trunks of those trees, images of unicorns frolicked, so fluid and lifelike Riony expected to see them come to life.

Her hand wrapped around the acorn pendant at her neck. Her eyes prickled with tears and she quickly blinked them away.

The refugees at the front of the group approached the doors, pushing at the heavy stone. It didn't budge, which Riony wasn't sure whether to find comforting or concerning.

It meant whatever was outside couldn't easily get in. Unfortunately, they were outside.

She moved forward to offer her strength to their efforts as well, but it was clear brute force wasn't getting them anywhere. Instead, they started shouting.

"Let us in!"

"We're out here! We have children out here!"

"Open the doors!"

It took a few long, nerve-wracking moments with no

response. And then the stone shifted. A little at first, and then the heavy stone rolled fully open.

Two guards met them at the door, checking for the threat of revenants before letting them through. The man and woman both had a glowing blue crystal hanging from a net on their belts.

"Whoa," Lyrrin gasped.

"More refugees," the female guard almost groaned. "I'll show them the way in."

The dark-skinned woman wore a mix of scrappy armor, pieced together from mismatched parts. She cupped her hands around her mouth and yelled, "Stick with me unless you can see in the dark! I'll take you all inside and you can sort yourselves out from there."

The guard turned and started walking without waiting on a reply.

Riony could only see a long, empty cave disappearing into the darkness in front of them.

There was a little hesitation, but with another prompting from the remaining guard, the group of refuges got moving, hurrying to keep up with the glow of light the guard carried away from them.

The cave seemed massive to Riony, large enough for

them all to walk along without coming up against the edges or ceiling, and the cyan light glinted off carvings running along the nearby walls as well. Lyrrin squeezed her hand, a skip in her step as they walked into the heart of the mountain.

The shifting grumble of the heavy doors closing behind them chased an echo along the caves.

Will we ever see the sun again?

Riony wasn't sure what to expect, preparing to live in a dark tunnel like the one they walked through like mice in a hole, but then the humming sounds of human life reached her and a brighter glow as they reached the end of the passage.

An immense cavern opened up before them. Stalagmites as big as castles shot toward the craggy ceiling, carved with doors and windows and stairs. People moved all around narrow streets filled with blue light from hundreds, thousands of crystals like the one the guard carried.

Riony smelled food. Riony heard laughter.

We made it.

A chittering sound made Riony flinch. Her gaze shot up, seeing the elegant swoop of small bats far above.

Lyrrin's eyes seemed to have doubled in size as she

looked out over the cool-blue, magically lit world before them.

Some of their group split off immediately, without a word to the others, with clear intention on where they were going, or simply needing to continue moving forward. Some took a moment to say goodbye. Others simply sat down on the dusty, ivory stone and cried as they looked out over the underground sanctuary.

Riony's heart pulled tight inside her, wanting to do the same.

They'd made it. They were safe.

Could we have been here, safe, with Amma and Pabba if we'd just left earlier?

Riony shook off all of the what-ifs that were playing out painful, imagined lives in her head, and nudged Lyrrin forward again.

As they moved passed the guard, she eyed up Riony and Lyrrin, travelling alone. "You'll find somewhere to stay at the Orphan's Den."

She pointed off to the right.

Riony scowled back in reply.

But that was what they were now.

And they did need somewhere to stay. At least until

Riony worked out how to earn them a living in this strange new environment. Then she would look after herself and Lyrrin alone. She couldn't trust anyone else to keep them safe. To keep Lyrrin's differences hidden.

Riony adjusted Lyrrin's hood to make sure it was covering the shimmer of bright blue hair-growth that had been coming through recently, since Riony hadn't been able to keep it dyed on their journey there.

They headed the way the guard pointed.

Their path led up and down, winding with the natural form of the caves and carved with elegant, sweeping staircases. People came in and out of homes within the stone, using huge round doors of rolling stone.

Merchants and beggars lined the open streets and the occasional musical *plink* of water dripping from the high ceiling into a clear pool sounded almost welcoming.

"What do people eat down here?" Lyrrin's voice was bright with enthusiasm. "Do you think they eat *worms*?"

Riony joined Lyrrin's disgusted giggle. "Pabba once pretended to eat a worm when I was gardening with him."

Lyrrin's face shifted, all mirth dropping away. She jerked her hand free of Riony's and grunted.

Riony's first impulse was to apologize for mentioning

their parents, for bringing with it the pain that caused. But she couldn't apologize for remembering them, for still loving them, for holding onto all those moments.

Riony took a deep breath through her nose and kept her tone light. "Mushrooms. They definitely eat mushrooms. Can you smell it?"

Lyrrin's hard expression softened and she placed a hand on her stomach. "I'm hungry."

"My too. Let's keep going. We'll see what food we can find."

Riony had found one single, silver sov shining in the dirt along their journey there. She fished it out, looking at the merchants they passed for a food that looked familiar.

The coin got them one big loaf to share and some change.

Riony tore the bread with her hands, and she and Lyrrin devoured it. There was a different, smokey flavor to the deep brown bread. Riony wasn't sure what it had been made with, but it was good and filled the ache in her stomach.

Across the street, a girl of around Riony's age watched them eat. When Riony caught her eye, she tucked caramel colored hair behind both ears, smiled, and stepped over

to them.

"Hey," the girl smiled sweetly at Riony. "Did you just come in with the new lot?"

Stars, she's pretty.

Riony wiped the last of the crumbs from her chin. "Uh, yeah."

"I can show you around if you like." The young woman reached a hand out, brushing it in a friendly greeting onto Riony's shoulder.

The way Kaya once had. A way that brought back too many memories. A way that felt like the harbinger of pain. A coldness seeped from Riony's heart, spreading throughout her.

Riony's lips twisted into a wicked smirk. "There's a lot I'd like to show you too. In bed. As soon as I have one for myself."

The young woman's face twisted in disgust. "What is sparking wrong with you?"

She backed away, turning her back on Riony and returning to her friends.

Riony's sly smile remained.

It was for the best.

There was only one thing Riony could focus on now.

One goal.

Keeping Lyrrin safe.

They had escaped the burned and revenant ravaged aboveground, but Riony knew she couldn't relax in this strange new underground world they had stepped into. One filled with strange magic and who knew what else.

One where she still had to find a way to keep the two of them fed and alive.

Alone.

Riony missed her parents with the strength of a dragon claw squeezing around her chest.

How am I supposed to do this without them?

Lyrrin stood on tip-toes, trying to touch one of the crystal lights held in a niche in the nearby wall.

"I like it here! The crystals are so pretty!"

Riony bent over, lowering herself closer to Lyrrin and smirking. "You don't mind the darkness?"

"I am not scared of the dark!"

Riony gently rolled her eyes. "I'm glad you like it here. This is our new home."

"No more walking? I'm so tired of all the walking!"

"We'll get a break from the walking soon. And no more revs. No more fire. We'll be safe here."

I hope we'll be safe here.

Riony stood up to her full height, looking out over the jumble of makeshift homes, dripping limestone, and sea of magical cyan light.

What is life going to be like here?

Riony didn't understand how the people here made the crystals glow, what ancient magic and secrets this new world they had come to held. What dangers it held.

She took Lyrrin's hand in hers again and kept her other rested on the hilt of her sword, and they continued into the echoing, cavernous undercity.

I'll do anything I have to do to make sure we are safe here.

Riony hoped she would be enough.

About the Author

Professional daydreamer, Selina A. Fenech writes "adorably dark" Epic and Urban Fantasy for teens and adults. Filled with sweet and quirky characters, laugh out loud moments, and perilous adventures, her magical worlds are perfect for readers who love daring twists and happily ever afters.

A cancer survivor determined to live life to the fullest, she is an escape room enthusiast, avid gardener, foodie and self-proclaimed geek, residing in Australia.

In addition to literature, Selina applies her unique take on the dichotomy of light and dark as a professional fantasy artist working under the name Selina Fenech and has published many illustrated books, oracle decks, and colouring books.

Find Out More About Selina

OFFICIAL WEBSITE: www.selinafenech.com

Memory's Wake Trilogy

A modern girl lost in and hunted in a fairy tale world.

An illustrated young adult portal fantasy with

Arthurian and Victorian themes.

Empath Chronicles

Teenagers with superpowers fueled by emotions ... what

could go wrong? A young adult superhero romance.

MORE BOOKS BY SELINA A FENECH

Beshadowed

You have been lied to. Werewolves, vampires, ghosts …
they aren't what you think. What is really lurking in the
dark? A spooky urban fantasy.

Fairy Tale Wishes

Enchanting and inclusive standalone fairy tale
retellings.

www.ingramcontent.com/pod-product-compliance
Lightning Source LLC
Chambersburg PA
CBHW032013180726
48283CB00008B/2662